WILD WILD WEST™

WILD WILD WEST ™

A junior novelization by Dina Anastasio

Story by Jim Thomas & John Thomas
Screenplay by S.S. Wilson & Brent Maddock and
Jeffrey Price & Peter S. Seaman

WARNER BROS. PRESENTS

A PETERS ENTERTAINMENT /SONNENFELD- JOSEPHSON PRODUCTION IN ASSOCIATION WITH TODMAN, SIMON, LeMASTERS PRODUCTIONS A BARRY SONNENFELD FILM WILL SMITH KEVIN KLINE
KENNETH BRANAGH SALMA HAYEK "WILD WILD WEST" MUSIC BY ELMER BERNSTEIN CO-PRODUCER GRAHAM PLACE EDITED BY JIM MILLER PRODUCTION DESIGNER BO WELCH DIRECTOR OF PHOTOGRAPHY MICHAEL BALLHAUS, A.S.C. EXECUTIVE PRODUCER BILL TODMAN, JR.,
JOEL SIMON, KIM LeMASTERS, TRACY GLASER, BARRY JOSEPHSON STORY BY JIM THOMAS & JOHN THOMAS SCREENPLAY BY S.S. WILSON & BRENT MADDOCK AND JEFFREY PRICE & PETER S. SEAMAN
www.wildwildwest.net PRODUCED BY JON PETERS AND BARRY SONNENFELD DIRECTED BY BARRY SONNENFELD

SCHOLASTIC INC.
New York   Toronto   London   Auckland   Sydney   Mexico City   New Delhi   Hong Kong

ISBN 0-439-08653-1

12 11 10 9 8 7 6 5 4 3 2 1   9/9 0 1 2 3 4/0

Printed in the U.S.A.
First Scholastic printing, July 1999

This book is for Liam Rowe

CHAPTER 1

Captain James T. West was shivering and quaking and his teeth were chattering and shaking. At first the water in the railroad water tower had been refreshing, but now it was turning him into a freezing prune. Clearly, it was time to get out. Man it was cold! Definitely time to get out!

West took one last glance through his lookout knothole and studied the West Virginia night sky. This hadn't turned out to be such a bad job after all. When the Civil War had ended four years before, in 1865, West was prepared for the worst. President

Lincoln might have freed the slaves, but life certainly wasn't going to be easy for blacks in America, even if you were a U.S. Army officer like Captain James T. West.

West had thought this post was going to be boring, but so far it had been anything but. It was always something — like . . . hey! What the! Uh-oh! Watch out! Right that minute the clatter of thundering wagon wheels could be heard outside his water tower lookout.

What was *this* coming down the dusty road! West shoved his eye against the hole and tried to make out what that rickety wagon was that was flying around the corner of the old tobacco warehouse and skidding to a stop below him. That six-horse team that had been dragging it sure seemed relieved that they could rest now, judging from all that snortin' and stompin'. Two rebels, the kind that had fought in the defeated

Confederate army were sliding off the buck-board now and stumbling into the ware-house.

West shivered again. Man, was it ever *freezing!* What were these guys up to! No good, that's what! But what sort of no good?

West peered down through the glass roof of the warehouse and considered his options. Those no good rebels, with the help of the warehouse guards, were carrying out boxes and loading them onto that rickety wagon. And now they were covering the boxes with a tarp.

"Next stop New Orleans!" they were saying.

What was up with rebels? How come rebels refused to believe the Civil War was over? How come they couldn't get it through their thick heads that their side had lost? West knew the rebels had chosen New Orleans as the new battleground. New Orleans — first stop toward the return of slavery. West knew exactly what these guys had in mind. They were determined to see the South rise again. But it wasn't going to happen. Not as long as Jim West was around.

There was one small problem. Captain James T. West was naked. He had left his clothes on the ground when he decided to cool off in the water tower, and they were still there, right next to the wagon. He'd have to climb down and grab them while the men were inside the warehouse, doing whatever it was they were doing.

One of the rebels was carrying a box out of the warehouse. Now he was slamming it onto the back of the wagon, spooking the horses and sending them up onto their hind legs, way up, making them scream with terror.

And hey, what was going on with that wagon wheel? The axle was caught on the

4

water tower leg — the very same water tower that Captain James T. West, *naked* Captain James T. West, was peeking out of. If those crazy horses got it in their minds to bolt, they would be taking the rotting wooden tower with them. And they'd be taking him too, without his clothes. *That* would be embarrassing!

The horses bolted. They neighed and snorted and took off. And just as West had predicted, the tower came crashing down . . . which made life sort of interesting for the naked captain.

The water blasted out of the upside-down tower and became a water slide, a slide on which West was soon riding. It took him out of the broken tower and over, around, and through the glass skylight and smashed him down onto a pile of boxes.

At least the next wave delivered his cowboy hat.

West snatched up the hat, pulled himself to his feet, and covered whatever he could with it. It had a good-sized brim, but it still didn't cover much. It didn't do much good. He needed his clothes. Where were his clothes?

One of the rebels was saying something about a naked somebody or other. He was using the "N" word — the word that West had spent four long years fighting never to hear again. West was not pleased. Nope! West didn't like that at all.

Captain James T. West was an expert at many things, but one of the things he was best at was martial arts. His kicks were notorious throughout the Union. He could mix it up with the best of them. He advanced quickly toward the intruders. *Whap!* The first rebel was down. *Whap!* The second. And then, suddenly, there were his clothes, riding a wave. West had no choice. He'd have to slam and shift and karate-chop his enemies and and maneuver into his clothes at the same time.

"Could I have a little privacy here?" West shouted as he tried to slide his leg into his pants.

But the bad guys kept coming, and West kept hopping and raising his leg and sending them down, one leg in, other leg up, sending these no good rebels flying onto their Southern butts.

When they were all down, West turned, just as the spooked horses went thundering past, dragging the fully-loaded wagon behind them.

Dressed now, West placed his hat on his head where it belonged, grinned, and threw himself at the wagon. The horses raced faster, dragging West's boots through the dirt, threatening to trample him, until, at last, he was up, up, up, on top of the wagon and his nose was pressing into one of the mysterious boxes.

Inside, something was clanking, clinking, and tinkling like chimes. It sounded like the box was filled with glass.

West took a closer look. He'd seen those bottles before. The glass vials were filled with nitroglycerine, which was one big powerful explosive, and he knew what that meant. These guys were planning on blowing something up, and West had a pretty good idea what they had in mind.

As the terrified horses flew along the dusty roads, Jim West grabbed the halter and yanked, harder, then harder still, as he tried to stop them. But they weren't having it. No way! Nothing stopping these animals!

Okay, he'd just have to think of a way to stop them! And he'd have to think of something fast. But that was no problem at all, because Captain James T. West was a fast kinda guy.

CHAPTER 2

"WHOA!" Captain James T. West shouted as the horses flew around a corner, taking the turn on two wheels. What was this! These galloping steeds were heading straight toward the edge of a steep chasm!

West's breath caught. His heart shot right up into his throat. The dusty road was disappearing. If those horses didn't quit their running, it was goodbye Captain West!

"I said WHOA!" West hollered one more time. He closed his eyes and crossed his toes and fingers.

The horses stopped.

West waited until his heart stopped pounding, then climbed down from the wagon and slapped the dust off his jacket. He checked the crease in his trousers, patted the horses, and looked around.

Behind him, in a huge old building, a party was booming. Above the din, a woman was singing.

West moved closer and listened. The woman's voice was drifting out through an open window. West went to the window and looked in. No beautiful woman that he could see. He couldn't see anything, in fact, because that huge hulking form was in the way. The big guy sure was ugly and he sure was familiar. West squinted, trying to make him out. Yes indeed, he had definitely seen *that* mountain of a man before.

"General Bloodbath McGrath!" West whispered.

West knew him well. He had fought against him on the battlefield. He had taken him down, defeated him, sent him packing. And now here he was again, a looming shadow framed in a window.

Old McGrath definitely had seen better days. His Confederate dress jacket was tattered and popping off his filthy, bloated body. And the ear! The famous ear! West had heard all about *that* ear.

General Bloodbath McGrath's ear had been hacked off in battle. And now look at him! Bloodbath the one-eared animal! But wait! It looked like McGrath's missing ear had been replaced by a small leather horn. It was repulsive!

"Sing, Dora!" McGrath was shouting. The woman sang louder, and moved toward the window. West could make her out now — she was a fancy one, all right. Huge hair and lots of makeup. A real party girl. McGrath must have liked her, because he was sweating and clapping his hands as she belted out her song, louder and louder.

Suddenly the singing stopped and Mc-Grath and the woman disappeared from the window.

West moved to another window and peered inside. The woman, Dora, was saying something about the clasp on her belt. Now McGrath was fiddling with it. And then . . .

The clasp popped open, and inside a small screen began to spiral, round and round, as McGrath's eyes locked onto it, following the spirals, round and round.

"Wha . . . what's this?" the general whispered.

"It's a deep, deep pool," Dora told him. "Maybe your old swimmin' hole. Getting sleepy, General?" She was attempting to hypnotize him — and it was working.

McGrath's eyes were rolling around in his head now. "Yes, I'm sleepy," he said groggily.

"Good," Dora said. "You're going to be my little doggie now. And when I say 'Speak,' you will tell me what I want to know. Understood?"

"*Woof!*" barked the general.

"All right, little doggie. Sit up."

The general sat up.

"I notice there is a sack in the room next door. Now you must tell me who's in that sack. Do you understand? Is it the scientist, Dr. Escobar? Speak!"

"*Woof! Woof!*" barked the general.

"Speak *words*, dumb doggie. You have kidnapped whoever is in that sack. Now, tell me the name of the man you kidnapped him for. Who ordered you to kidnap him?"

But the general had stopped barking. He wasn't saying anything at all, because the spiral was slowing. McGrath was coming out of his trance.

The general began to growl. He reached out and grabbed at Dora's dress, but Dora was too busy fiddling with the failed spiral to notice. She didn't notice the knife that he was holding, either. She didn't notice that he was pointing the knife at her. But West did.

Just as McGrath was about to stop Dora's fiddling forever, Captain James T. West exploded through the window and kicked the knife out of McGrath's hand.

West rolled to his feet, glanced down at Dora, and grinned.

"Didn't mean to startle you, ma'am," he said. "Looks like you could use some help."

Surprised, the woman took a moment to recover, then smiled sweetly up at West.

"Looks can be deceivin'," she cooed. "I'm fine."

"I can see that," West said. "So you can run along now. I'll take care of McGrath."

West turned and started to lunge at McGrath, but the woman stopped him.

"No!" she cried. "I need him!"

Suddenly McGrath recognized West and let out a rebel yell so loud that the whole building heard him.

"WEST!" he shouted, and throughout the house doors opened and slammed and McGrath's men raced toward their leader's call.

In the next room, General McGrath's companion, a tall Native American named Hudson, heard the call and jumped. He had been guarding the man in the sack. Dora had been right — it *was* Dr. Escobar, the scientist they had kidnapped. Hudson knew just what he had to do.

"Get Escobar out of here!" he ordered his henchmen.

But as the men lifted the wiggling, jiggling sack, a fierce-looking Dora appeared in the doorway and raised her bracelet-laden arm. The bracelets clattered as Dora clicked a lock. Instantly, one of them opened to reveal a pair of custom handcuffs.

Hudson wasn't at all ready to be taken. He reached for his gun. Dora saw it and pulled out a perfume bottle filled with mace.

She squeezed out a quick spray, then smiled as Hudson dropped to his knees and held out his wrists, defeated, ready to be hand-cuffed.

Dora was about to snap on the cuffs when something smashed into her back and sent her flying.

West, it seemed, was stronger than he looked. While trying to stop McGrath's escape, he had used his best drop kick to send the huge, hulking general flying straight into the next room — and into Dora's back.

Hey! What was this! Suddenly, there were henchmen everywhere, holding Dora, drop-kicking West, allowing Hudson to escape with the kidnapped scientist, Escobar.

"Get outta my way, lady!" West shouted at Dora as McGrath managed to get away too. "I'm from the U.S. Army!"

"And I'm not a lady!" Dora shouted back, in a voice that sounded *very much* like a man's! "I'm a U.S. marshall, *disguised* as a lady.

The name is Artemus Gordon. Now get out of *my* way!"

As U.S. Marshall Artemus Gordon whipped off his wig and presented his badge, Captain James T. West blinked. They stared at each other without speaking.

Outside, the dark night was suddenly quiet, except for the soft whisper of a woman's voice. The woman was standing beside the wagon that West had been riding on not long before. The six horses had been let loose and were gone now. But the boxes filled with nitroglycerine were still there, ready to explode at any moment, if touched in the wrong way.

The woman's name was Lippenreider, so called because she was an expert at reading lips. At that moment she was holding a pair of opera glasses, and reading the lips of West and Gordon.

"They're both saying the same thing, Dr.

Loveless. They're both saying 'Get out of my way! Get out of my way!' 'U.S. Army.' 'U.S. marshall.'"

Dr. Loveless sighed and moved his wheelchair closer to his lip reader. Perhaps she had misunderstood. He didn't like the sound of U.S. Army or U.S. marshall.

Lippenreider was about to continue when the quiet black night was disturbed by the sound of approaching henchmen. They were carrying the sack that contained the kidnapped scientist, Dr. Escobar.

"Federal agents inside, sir," Hudson reported breathlessly to his boss.

"So Miss Lippenreider informs me," Dr. Loveless told him. "Still, I believe good manners dictate that we should send out . . ."

Dr. Loveless's underlings waited in silence as he raised his cane. They smiled as the cane telescoped out. Long now, the cane poked at the linchpin on the wagon, sending

it, and the boxes of nitro on top, rolling —
straight toward the building.

As the wagon picked up speed, Hudson,
Dr. Loveless, and his henchmen, along with
the kidnapped scientist, climbed into a waiting carriage and sped off in the opposite direction.

The nitro-wagon rolled through the
night, faster and faster, as West and Gordon,
oblivious to the impending danger, continued
to argue.

"So now what?" West was asking.

He didn't have to wait long for an answer. Within seconds, the nitro-wagon
smashed into the side of the building and,
with a blast that abruptly ended their con-
versation, exploded.

CHAPTER 3

At the last possible second, West had heard the wagon coming. He was familiar with the sound of those wagon wheels, and he knew all too well what was on it. One second before the nitro had disintegrated the building, West had thrown himself and Gordon through the building, into the dark night.

And now here he was, a week later, alive and intact, in the middle of Washington, D.C.

Captain James T. West leaned forward in his saddle and adjusted his cowboy hat. Beneath him, his magnificent black stallion was racing down Pennsylvania Avenue past

20

horse-drawn carriages and those newfangled contraptions called bicycles. When he reached the White House, he reined in his steed and patted its long damp neck. Then he slid down onto the dusty road, tied the horse to a hitching post, and winced.

Something was wrong with his leg. Somewhere in last week's melee he must have done it some serious damage. He'd have to work on those drop kicks. Couldn't afford an injured leg these days.

West put some weight on the leg and limped through the front door of the White House. He was heading toward the Oval Office when four house detectives appeared in front of him and blocked his way.

"Whoa there, pardner," one of them hissed, looking down his self-important nose. "You can't just traipse into the President's office, cowboy. Now gimme the gun."

The detective nodded at the six-shooter on West's hip. West was fiddling with his six-shooter, trying to stall, when a booming voice from the Oval Office door stopped him.

"Gentlemen!" The voice echoed off the White House walls.

The detectives turned, then began to back away.

President Ulysses S. Grant nodded toward West.

"Don't make Captain West any later for his appointment than he already is!" he said as the men turned and quickly retreated.

West grinned and walked toward the President. He knew President Grant well. West had served under him when Grant was the supreme commander of the Union Army, and since he had become President, Grant had called upon him often.

West followed Grant into the Oval Office and waited as the large bearded man lit a cigar.

"Sorry about that," Grant said. "There's

been a lot of death threats lately. They made me hire some damn detectives. How about a drink, or a cigar?"

"Thank you, sir," West said as he limped across the room toward the bar. He poured himself a glass of whiskey and chose a cigar from the humidor.

"I hear you let General McGrath get away," the President announced when West was settled.

West bit down on the cigar, tension filling his body. "Sir," he said. "I had him right in my hands when some half-a-sissy wearin' a dress ruined . . ."

"You mean Artemus Gordon." The big man studied his cigar.

"You know him?" West was incredulous.

"Of course I know him. He's the best marshall I've got! He's a genius!"

As West listened, amazed, the President continued.

"Gordon has proven himself time and

again as a very cunning operator with a rapacious intellect. Nothing will stop him from completing a mission for his President, except, perhaps, the impulsive actions of a headstrong cowboy!"

Wait one minute! West thought. He couldn't believe what he was hearing. And then he *didn't* believe what he was hearing. Something was very wrong here.

West pulled himself up to his full height and glared at the President.

"Who are you?" he asked, in a cold, slow voice.

"I am the President of the United States," the big man announced.

"Wrong answer! Who are you?"

"I am the President of . . ."

As West drew his gun, the big man seemed to shrink. "I'm Artemus Gordon," he admitted at last. The master of disguise had pulled off another one — almost.

"Well, you certainly aren't the President."

"How did you know?" Gordon asked.

West slid his gun back into its holster and nodded at Gordon's Harvard class ring.

"The President went to West Point," he said. "Not Harvard."

Gordon was about to say a few words about Harvard being a better something or other when a giant voice interrupted him.

"Will somebody please tell me what this is all about!"

West and Gordon turned toward the doorway of the Oval Office and shrugged sheepishly. The *real* President Grant was standing there, his huge frame filling the doorway. He was surrounded by his house detectives.

Slowly, nervously, Gordon began to peel off his fake nose and his padded cheeks.

"Uh, sir," he said quickly, rambling as he

turned himself from Grant back into Gordon, "in perilous times like these, I was, uh, simply illustrating how you could actually walk right into the very bowels of the White House."

"You're clever, Gordon," the real President said. "A very clever actor. Talented, too. But one day it'll get you killed."

As West glanced over at Gordon, smirking, the President continued.

"And you, West, not every situation calls for your patented approach — shoot first, shoot later, shoot again, and *then,* when they're all dead, try to ask a question or two."

Having chastised both of them, President Grant shook his head and sighed.

"Working together will be good for both of you."

West and Gordon stared straight ahead, their eyes widening at the horror of that suggestion.

"But sir!" they cried as one. "I work . . ." Each was about to say "alone." But neither got the chance.

"You work the way your Commander-in-Chief tells you to work," President Grant announced as West and Gordon glared at each other.

"Now, if you'll follow me to the War Room," the President said, "I will explain exactly what I mean."

CHAPTER 4

President Grant walked into the War Room briskly, followed by West and Gordon. The huge room was a buzz of activity. The newest telegraph machines were clicking and clacking out important messages. Printing machines were grinding out pages of the latest reports. And maps of every corner of the world covered the walls.

The President stopped at a display of black-and-white photos that were attached to a far wall and cleared his throat. The photos showed several distinguished-looking

28

men, all wearing whiskers and wise expressions.

"These are ten of our country's best scientists," the President explained. "All of them have been kidnapped in the last year, by General McGrath."

West and Gordon straightened and watched the President, waiting.

President Grant continued, "The fact is, gentlemen, you've both been working on the same case all along. I wonder why it took you so long to realize it. According to this letter, we have only one week before . . . Wait. Let me read it."

Grant smoothed out a piece of paper and began to read.

"General Grant. The scientists that you seek are in my employ. They are working to create a weapons system beyond the pale of contemporary imagination. History and

justice are on my side. I suggest you put your affairs in order. You have one week before you will surrender the U.S. Government."

The President sighed and refolded the letter. Then he nodded to an aide, who handed him a glass case in which there was a cake shaped like the White House.

"This letter was delivered inside this cake," Grant informed West and Gordon.

"Hmmm," Gordon said, reaching toward the cake. "I know that flavor. It's marzipan, isn't it?"

"Wait!" the President cried, grabbing his hand.

Gordon gasped and yanked his hand away as dozens of deadly-looking spiders swarmed out from inside the tasty-looking cake.

"It's McGrath, sir," West announced. "McGrath, who wishes the South to rise again. McGrath will do anything to see the South as it was before the war. I'm gonna stop him . . ."

"Sir!" Gordon interrupted. "West's obsession aside, McGrath may be a vicious killer, but a mastermind he is not. Someone else is behind this plot to overthrow the U.S. Government. But whom do we seek? After consulting with Intelligence . . ."

"Sir!" West said, cutting Gordon off in mid-sentence. "McGrath's headed for New Orleans, where he will begin his offensive. The longer we stand here talkin', the farther away he gets. I don't need 'intelligence' to tell me that!"

The look on President Grant's face indicated that he had had enough.

"Gentlemen!" he said firmly. "I'm leaving today for Utah. As you may know, the Union Pacific Railroad has been laying tracks westward from Nebraska. At the same time, the Central Pacific Railroad has been put-

31

ting down tracks eastward from California. These tracks are to meet soon at Promontory Point in Utah, creating the United States' first transcontinental railroad. For the first time, the United States will be truly united."

President Grant held up the letter and stared, hard, at the two men before him.

"Someone wants us divided. Now look. You two are the best I've got. Put aside your differences and stop this madman . . . whoever he is. If you fail, well, we may never know how great this country could've been."

The President snapped off a salute, and West and Gordon returned it, "Remember," Grant said. "You have a week. Dismissed!"

A week! West and Gordon thought about that as the President stomped out of the room.

When he was gone, an aide approached the two men. "The President has put a private train at your disposal," he told them. "It's Engine Number Five, on Track Six."

Then, as West moved toward the doorway, the aide presented Gordon with a wrapped box. "Mr. Gordon," he said. "Here is the item you requested."

Gordon took the box and hurried after West. When they were outside, West marched over to the hitching post and started to untie his leaping horse. He glowered at Gordon as the actor — master of disguise, inventor, and U.S. Marshall — wandered over to a bush and retrieved a bicycle. The rubber wheel on the front of the bike was huge, almost thirty-six inches in diameter. And the wheel on the back was tiny — only a third the size of the front wheel.

Captain James T. West took in Gordon's bicycle and shook his head in disgust. Gordon was going to ride *that* to the train?

"I call it the Bi-axle Nitro-Cycle —" Gordon began.

"Save it!" West called, swinging up onto his snorting, wild horse. "I've got a train to catch."

"Yee-haaa!" West hollered as he shot Gordon a neat salute and gave his horse a quick kick with his spurs.

As the horse took off, Gordon calmly attached the wrapped box onto the seat of his Bi-Axle Nitro bike. He was in no hurry. There was no need for that. He climbed onto the bike lazily. Then he took out a fresh, clean hankie and cleaned a pair of goggles.

When he was finally ready, Gordon let out a loud shout, and started up . . . Smoke poured from the fiery exhaust as U.S. Marshall Artemus Gordon bolted forward and sped down the street at sixty miles per hour, *passing* Captain West on the way!

Hey! What was this! Neither West, *nor*

his nervous stallion, could believe it. The jittery horse reared up as West hung on for dear life.

Gordon, it seemed, had invented his very own motorcycle, fifteen years before an Englishman named Edward Butler attached an engine to a tricycle and went down in the record books.

Chapter 5

The train that President Grant had put at West and Gordon's disposal was called the *Wanderer*. The brand-new steam engine and two gleaming passenger cars were watched over, and indeed *loved*, by a grizzly old man named Coleman. The *Wanderer* was Coleman's pride and joy.

In his coal-stained suit, his white hair flying, Coleman eased his train out of the C Street Station with the utmost care. Gordon was on board, and Coleman assumed that West was, too.

He was wrong. For West, it seemed, had missed their appointed departure time.

The *Wanderer* left on time. Always.

So intent was Coleman on his job that he did not hear West thundering past him in a desperate effort to catch up.

"Stop this train!" West hollered as he pushed the last ounce of energy from his exhausted horse. "Do you hear me? Stop this train!"

The train continued to pick up speed.

Seated in the parlor car, U.S. Marshall Artemus Gordon heard West's call, but he did not look up from his *sewing*. Ignoring West's cry, he continued to stitch the material that he was holding in his lap.

"Stop the train!" West hollered again.

But still Gordon did not look up.

Desperately, West leaned over the side of his galloping horse and grabbed the handle on the side of the train. When he had it firmly in his grasp, he swung out of the saddle and hung on for dear life.

This would never do. He needed a step, a

place to rest his boot, a way onto the speeding train. He held on, searching for that step, and at last he found it . . . a small metal plate that became his lifeline.

As West dropped through a sliding partition in the roof, Gordon finally looked up from his sewing.

"Thanks for dropping in," he deadpanned.

West fell into one of the plush club chairs and glowered at Gordon. Beside him, crystal decanters and glasses tinkled. Bookcases filled with books trembled. But West did not notice. He did not notice the long pool table, or the fine linen. He was too hot, too dusty, too angry.

"Put down the needlepoint and let's settle this like men!" West challenged.

Gordon held up some real needlepoint — not the sewing that West had been referring to. "As a matter of clarification," he

said, "*this* is what needlepoint looks like.
"What you see in my lap is not needlepoint.
Right now, I am putting the final touches on
a new invention of my creation. I call it . . .
The Impermeable. It's a vest that, when worn
under clothing, can stop any modern bullet
fired, even at close range."

"Oh really?" West said as he drew his
gun and pointed it at Gordon's gut.

Gordon pulled the vest away from his
stomach and held it up. "Uh, well," he said, a
little nervous. "It hasn't really been tested
empirically yet."

"Get up!" West ordered.

"Guns," Gordon sighed. "I find guns so
primitive and unnecessary."

"Oh, yeah? Well, how do you feel about
fists?"

Gordon yawned and put down his latest
invention. Then, with a weary sigh, he rose to
his feet and looked down at West.

"I must tell you, Mr. West, I've always felt that allowing a situation to degenerate into physical violence is a failure on my part."

West rose to his feet and glared. "Well then, Mr. Gordon, you have failed!"

Whap! West threw a lightning punch that drove Gordon across the train car. Surprised, but not badly hurt, Gordon put his hands together and raised his leg like a stork.

"I'm sorry, Mr. West," Gordon said as he kicked a switch. "You have brought this on yourself."

When the switch clicked, a leather hammer swung down from the ceiling and whacked West on the side of the head. West flew backward, and landed on the pool table.

West sat up, shook himself, and was about to attack again when Gordon calmly poked a hidden button. The pool table spun around, and suddenly West was gone.

40

Gordon grinned. "I love this train," he muttered.

The pool table had flipped the astounded West through the floorboards.

Underneath the speeding *Wanderer*, West, eyes wide with surprise and terror, was hanging on for dear life, just inches above the track.

Above him, Gordon was pouring himself a glass of fine Bordeaux wine and speaking to the floor.

"The President asked for my suggestions on how to make the *Wanderer* both comfortable and functional," he was saying.

Grasping for a handhold, West yanked at the tubes and wires on the underside of the train, loosening a tube directly below Gordon . . . which caused shackles to snap out of the arms of Gordon's chair and pin his wrists . . . as the floor opened below him and the chair disappeared . . . then reappeared, upside-down, under the train, directly next to his partner.

"Perhaps the President was right about us putting aside our petty differences," Gordon suggested.

West would have continued the discussion, but suddenly they both flipped and spun, and found themselves, once again, seated inside the parlor car.

Facing them, in his coal-stained suit, was the grizzly old man, Coleman. His eyes were filled with fire and his hands held a large copper pot.

"Knock each other about all ya please," he growled. "But harm my train and I'll douse ya like dogs."

West and Gordon watched him sheepishly.

"Well then," Coleman said. "Let's get down to business, shall we gentlemen? Now, where to?"

"New Orleans," West answered instantly.

"I'm not so sure about that," Gordon said. "Perhaps we should let Professor Morton decide."

West stared at Gordon and frowned. What was this? "Who's Professor Morton?" he asked.

Gordon turned and strolled to the end of the car. "If you will follow me to the lab car, I will introduce you to the good professor. He may have lost his head, but I think he has a great deal to teach us."

CHAPTER 6

"**Y**ou may be wondering what was inside the wrapped box," Gordon announced as they entered the lab car.

West shuddered as Gordon pointed to a vise in front of them. It held . . . a decapitated head!

"Meet Professor Thaddeus Morton, expert in the field of metallurgy."

"That's a man's head!" West gasped.

"Indeed it is. The professor's head was discovered in a field of alfalfa. He had been kidnapped from the Massachusetts Institute of Technology six months ago."

"That's a man's head!" West gasped again.

"And a very brilliant head it was, which of course was the reason he was kidnapped. And this magnetic collar was around it when his body was discovered. I have yet to figure out why."

West couldn't help himself. He was too horrified to think straight.

"That's a man's head!" he repeated.

Gordon wasn't listening. He was busy fiddling with a lantern that was positioned behind the head.

"According to the Retinal Terminus Theory, a dying person's last conscious image is burned into the back of the eyeball like a photograph. Perhaps there's a clue there."

Barely able to contain himself, Gordon flipped the switch on the lantern that was attached to the dead man's head. If the theory worked, he would soon learn the very last thing that Professor Morton saw before he died.

Beams of light shone through the Professor's eyeballs and appeared on the wall. The softly colored image was blurry.

"Morton's last image," Gordon announced.

"That's a man's *head!*" West groaned yet again.

But after a moment, West calmed down and turned his own head slightly, in order to view the inverted image on the wall.

As he studied it, Gordon began to understand the problem. "Ah!" he said. "The refraction of the lenses causes the image to appear upside down. We simply . . ."

Gently, Gordon flipped Morton's head in the vise and studied the image on the wall once again.

The blurry image, now right side up, began to clear. West and Gordon squinted and watched as a picture of a man wearing a tiny horn for an ear appeared.

"It's McGrath!" West exclaimed. "I told you!"

But Gordon wasn't listening. He was too busy studying the picture of McGrath.

"Wait a minute!" he said. "He seems to have something in his pocket. What is it? It's too fuzzy to tell. Mortification of the aqueous humor seems to have led to the loss of . . ."

"I'll bet the guy needs glasses!" West announced, finishing the sentence for him.

West turned to the box, pulled out what were obviously Professor Morton's bifocal glasses, and placed them on the head's nose. When they were in place, West gestured toward the wall.

The white blur in McGrath's pocket, a piece of paper, was clear and focused now. It appeared to be an invitation. West read it aloud.

"Friends of the South! Come to a Surprise

Costume Ball. April 14, eight-thirty. 346 Garden Street . . ."

"Like I said," West laughed smugly. "New Orleans."

Today's date was April 7th. They had one week.

As the *Wanderer* chugged toward the New Orleans train station, Gordon thought about what to wear to this costume party. The options were unlimited.

On the other hand, Captain James T. West was not at all interested. "Jim West does not wear a costume!" he announced.

"But it's a *costume* party and we haven't been invited," Gordon reminded him. "What's your plan?"

"I go in. I kill McGrath. I buy a farm."

Gordon groaned and looked into his wardrobe. "No!" he said. "We go in. We work together. *We* surreptitiously gather intelligence so we can find and rescue the scientists. For that we need disguises."

Gordon glanced over at his partner. West was busy strapping on his six-shooters.

"If you *insist* on a firearm, how about this?" Gordon held up a belt with a silver buckle. As he tapped the buckle, a derringer pistol popped out. Then he pulled out a sequined dress and held the gun and the dress up together. "This gown would accessorize nicely with the gun, don't you think?"

"Hey, Gordon," West hissed as he stared hard into Gordon's face, "I'd rather be *dead!*"

Captain James T. West turned on his heels and stomped out of the car. He would go to the party alone, and he would definitely not be wearing a costume!

CHAPTER 7

The party at the huge New Orleans mansion was in full swing when West arrived. Rebels dressed in all kinds of outrageous costumes stepped from their horse-drawn carriages and made their way to the front door. Their minds were filled with grand ideas about how to help the South rise again. Their pockets were filled with money for the cause. Their checkbooks were ready.

These Southerners wanted the old life back. It had been good — to them. They needed their slaves. And at that moment they would do or pay anything to get that lifestyle back.

Jim West was idealistic — not stupid. He knew that he would not be a welcome visitor. The color of his skin would not be appreciated in the least. As the carriage *under* which he was hitching a ride pulled up at the mansion, he rolled into the shadows of the house and tried his best to be invisible. It worked — not even for a minute.

A guard spotted him.

"You've got about as much of a chance of havin' an invitation as a statue!" the guard sneered.

But West was too quick for him. Within seconds, the guard was down and West was climbing over the fence. Using the butt of his gun, he poked a hole in a glass door and let himself in. He made his way silently through the back of the house. Soon he found himself in an upstairs hallway.

Cautiously, trying not to be seen, he crept through the shadows to the balcony and looked over. Below, the party was in full swing. Loud music was pouring from the speakers as men and women in bizarre costumes danced and milled about.

"Well, well, an authentic cowboy outfit, complete with six guns," a voice behind West said huskily. "What a terribly clever costume, Mr. . . . ?"

West turned and faced a Chinese woman who was dressed as the Dragon Lady.

"West," he said. "Jim West."

"That's funny. I'm East. Mae Lee East. West meets East." The Dragon Lady held out her hand. "Are you here alone, Mr. West?"

West took her hand and grinned. "Actually, I'm trying to surprise my old friend General McGrath," he said. "Have you seen him around anywhere?"

"I don't believe that name was on our guest list, Mr. West. And I would know. I'm Dr. Loveless's personal assistant."

Whoa! West had heard *that* name before. Dr. Arliss Loveless. Was this his house? Was this his party?

"Dr. Arliss Loveless?" he asked. "One of the great founders of the Confederacy with Jefferson Davis? Funny how most people think he's dead."

The Dragon Lady smiled knowingly. "Tonight is his coming-out party," she said as she took his arm and led him down the stairs to the celebration.

West hesitated and studied the guests.

"See anyone that looks familiar?" Miss East asked.

West stepped forward and scanned the room. At first he did not recognize anyone, but when a woman with big hair walked past he pointed and said, "As a matter of fact, I do."

He'd seen *that* woman before. It was Soiled Dove, alias Artemus Gordon in a costume strikingly similar to the one he'd worn the first time West met him. Gordon, West surmised, must have decided to come as his favorite female.

Miss East watched him study the woman with the big hair. She began to sulk. "I'm jealous," she teased as she turned and blew him a small kiss. "Meet me later, in the foyer."

Miss East, the Dragon Lady, moved away and joined a group of women across the room. She raised her arms, and the women, singing together, belted out a rousing rendition of that anthem of the North, "The Battle Hymn of the Republic."

Okay, that's weird! West thought. *A bunch of Southerners singing the North's favorite song?*

Their voices grew louder and louder as an elevator beside them burst open and a man dressed as Abraham Lincoln appeared, riding on a mini-float. The float chugged out and moved slowly into the party. As it passed, Miss East and the other women tossed grapes on the floor around the float, singing, *"He has trampled down the vintage where the grapes of wrath are stored."*

West gaped in awe as the float rolled past. What was moving it? And then he noticed the wheels beneath the float. They were wheelchair wheels. He was pondering this curious fact when, suddenly, Abraham Lincoln exploded like a piñata, and Dr. Arliss Loveless appeared.

"Don't you just HATE that song?" Loveless announced with an impish grin.

The crowd grew silent as they took in the transformation of Lincoln to Loveless, who was, of course, supposed to be dead.

Loveless's grin grew wider.

"Why, y'all look like you've seen a ghost," he laughed. "It's me, dear friends, alive and kicking! Well, alive, anyway."

As he giggled, his staff moved in and removed the rest of his Lincoln costume.

The crowd gasped, then grew silent again. Loveless, it seemed, had not died, but he *had* been severely wounded. The bottom half of his body was missing.

Loveless chuckled as he took in the crowd's reaction from his wheelchair platform.

"We may have lost the war," he announced. "But we have not lost our sense of humor. Not even when we have lost half a body do we lose our sense of humor."

The room was eerily silent as Loveless turned to some guests who appeared to be foreign dignitaries.

"I owe a deep debt of gratitude to my friends across the sea for their comfort and succor. So, *mi casa es su casa!* My house is your house! Let the party begin!"

As Loveless signaled the musicians to continue playing, Miss East leaned down and whispered something in his ear. After a moment, he wheeled over to West.

"Mr. West," he drawled menacingly, "how good of you to come. It's nice to add a little *color* to the proceedings."

West cringed, but kept a lid on his temper. Instead, he forced a chuckle.

"Well, when a man comes back from the dead, it's an occasion to *stand* and be counted," he traded insult for insult.

Dr. Loveless smiled slightly. "Miss East informs me that you were expecting to meet General McGrath here. I haven't seen him in a long time. Perhaps Miss East will keep you from being a *slave* to your disappointment."

West shrugged. "Well," he said, "you know beautiful women. *They cut the legs* right out from under you."

Loveless's faced dropped. Clearly, he no longer thought this was funny. Miss East winked at West, then moved with Loveless in the direction of the study.

CHAPTER 8

West was clearly not invited to follow them. He did anyway, trying his best not to be seen by anyone. As he approached the study, his suspicions were confirmed. General McGrath was waiting outside.

Quickly, avoiding McGrath, West ducked behind someone in a mountain man costume carrying a French flag. The mountain man tried to slip away, but West stayed with him, peeking out to see what McGrath and Loveless were up to.

The two rebels disappeared into the study and closed the door. Clearly, an impor-

58

tant meeting was taking place behind that closed door, and West was determined to find out what it was all about.

As he made his way to the study door, West noticed the woman with the big hair — Soiled Dove — hovering nearby. Gordon must have noticed Loveless and McGrath disappear into the study too. West wasn't happy about having Gordon around, so once again he hid behind the mountain man until his nosy partner had disappeared. When she/he was gone, West hurried to the study door and looked through the keyhole.

"Peeking through the keyholes?" the mountain man chuckled, behind him. "So eighteenth-century."

West grunted and kept his eye focused on what was happening on the other side of the door.

"Dr. Loveless," McGrath was saying. "My men are ready to resume the war, but they have no weapons. Ever since the nitro and the guns were destroyed that night in the club, my men have been demoralized."

"Your men will have their weapons tonight," Dr. Loveless assured him. "And they shall have my promise that they will be part of the greatest military victory of this century. The South *shall* rise again!"

The worried look on McGrath's face changed to a relieved grin. "Oh, you're a pip, sir," he purred. "I'd follow you into the maw of Cerberus himself."

Loveless took a pencil from the desk and began to draw something on a piece of paper. Still peeking through the peephole, West tried to make it out. It appeared to be a map.

"Ah," Loveless was saying. "You *shall* follow me. Have your men here at ten o'clock tonight." Loveless leaned over and drew a large X on the map.

On the other side of the study door, West tried to make out the location of that X. Where, he wondered, were the rebels planning on meeting?

Loveless and McGrath left the desk and moved toward the study door. They were coming out! West pulled away from the keyhole and hid as they emerged. He waited until they were lost in the throng of partygoers.

When the coast was clear, West took a thin lock pick out of the band of his cowboy hat and moved toward the study door. He leaned down, glanced over his shoulder to make sure that no one was watching, then slipped the lock pick into the lock. He turned it to the left, then to the right, and finally it clicked. The door opened, and in a second he was inside.

In a corner of the hallway, the mountain man was watching. He did not seem that interested. As the study door closed behind West, the mountain man shrugged and turned away.

Inside the study, West was moving toward the desk. He knew exactly what he was looking for, and it wouldn't take more than a minute to find it.

When he reached the desk, he studied the blotter. Just as he had thought, the map itself was gone, but Loveless had left behind an impression of the map in the blotter. West took out his penknife and a pencil and quickly scraped some of the graphite from the pencil point onto the outline of the map.

But he wasn't quick enough. He was about to do a rubbing of the map when the paper he was using was suddenly swiped from his hand.

West glanced up. Dr. Loveless's personal assistant, Miss East, was standing beside him. She was holding the paper and watching him with a "naughty, naughty" look on her face.

"I thought I told you to meet me in foyer, Mr. West," she said.

"Oh, the foy-aay," West chuckled. "I've never been much good at French."

Miss East, it seemed, was not really interested in what West had to say. She had other things in mind, mainly moving his attention away from the blotter.

West grinned as she pushed him down into Loveless's chair and tried to kiss him. She was clever, all right, but West had a plan of his own. Slowly, carefully, he pushed her onto the desk so that her bare back rested on the blotter.

As she gazed into his eyes, listening to his hypnotic words of love, the tough Miss East began to soften. Unaware of West's devious mission, she became lost in the moment.

Ah, the romance of it all! When West had accomplished what he had set out to, he raised her up and glanced over her shoulder. His plan had worked, almost. The imprint of

as on her back, all right, but it was
backward and far too hard to read. He
would have to do something. But what?

Now here was a plan! A mirror! He
needed a mirror! He looked around, studying the room, then saw one, and backed Miss
East closer, and closer, until he could make
out the map on her back.

The image was clear now. The meeting
place, it appeared, was to be at Malheureux
Point, northeast of New Orleans.

Quickly, West disengaged himself from
Miss East and hurried out of the study. As
he slipped through the dancing crowd, he
noticed Soiled Dove and grabbed her. He
couldn't resist the temptation to brag a little
to his partner.

West swaggered a bit and strutted a bit,
and when the music changed and a reel
began to play, they danced a bit. What was
this! Soiled Dove wasn't paying the slightest

attention to him. The least Gordon could do was look him in the eye.

"I'm real impressed by the way you've got the dance floor staked out," West whispered, his words dripping with sarcasm. "Maybe one of your missing scientists will cut in on us. And by the way, I thought you should know that while you were trying to decide what shoes to wear tonight, I found out that our host, Dr. Loveless, is meeting McGrath and his troops at Malheureux Point in an hour."

West twirled Soiled Dove around and grinned. "So," he gloated, "you enjoy the party. I'm gonna go save the Republic."

Soiled Dove's eyes widened in surprise. She did not speak. She just stared at him, incredulous.

West turned on his heel and was about to leave the room when he strutted back and grinned at his partner again. "That costume of yours looks pretty good tonight," he said as he stretched out his hands and pinched her all over.

But Soiled Dove, it seemed, didn't think that was the least bit funny. She let out a scream that echoed off every wall in the house. And then she smacked him across the face as hard as she could.

West jumped back, shocked and upset. What was this? Didn't Gordon know that they were in a room full of rebels who had fought hard to keep their slaves? Didn't Gordon know that the rebels would use any excuse to hang a man of his color? Didn't Gordon know that the best excuse they could ask for, in this year 1869, was a black man annoying a white woman?

West glanced around him. The party had stopped. The room was silent. They stared. They glared. It was quite clear. Every single person in that room was ready to hang him.

No one said a word. Not yet. Not until

the mountain man stepped forward and said it for them.

"Hang him!" the mountain man shouted as he opened his deerskin jacket and pulled out a long, thick rope.

The mountain man tossed the rope to the angry crowd and chuckled.

Suddenly West understood. He knew that laugh. He knew that voice. It was *Gordon*! Gordon was dressed as a mountain man — not a woman! Soiled Dove was a real woman. And, uh, Captain James T. West was in big trouble.

West glared an "I'll get you for this" glare at Gordon as the mob yanked him out of the room.

Gordon turned away, ignoring West's pleading gaze, and moved off in the opposite direction. His plan had worked. The entire party was so intent on hanging West that they had left the mansion deserted.

As West was led away, Artemus Gordon

climbed the unguarded stairs and moved down an empty hallway toward a locked door. He leaned over, pulled out one of his newest inventions, an autowind lock pick, and opened the door.

CHAPTER 9

While his partner was making his way into the upstairs bedroom in search of the missing scientists, West was beginning to panic. He was far too young to die, wasn't he? And why had Gordon been so quick to offer the rebels the rope that was, at this very moment, being placed around his neck like a noose? As someone in the mob tossed the other end of the noose around a lamp-post, West's body tightened with fear and hatred. Where *was* Gordon?

West struggled with the ropes that bound his hands and feet and glared at the man who was lifting him onto the back of a wagon. The man was dressed as George Washington, which made West smirk, until he remembered where he was and what was about to happen to him. The Father of his Country — ha!

"George Washington" gave the driver a signal and the wagon moved forward an inch, tightening the noose around West's neck.

"Would it help if I said that I thought that woman I was annoying was a man?" West choked.

A woman in the crowd screamed and fainted. West glanced down at her. Oops. It was the real Soiled Dove.

Where is *Gordon?!* West thought, frantic, as the wagon inched forward a bit more and the noose tightened.

"Hang him!" George Washington shouted.

The wagon lurched forward and West's feet plummeted toward the ground.

What the . . . !!

As West hung there, his toes brushing the dirt, it took him a moment to understand what had just happened. And something *had* indeed happened, because . . .

He wasn't dead! He wasn't dying! In fact, he wasn't even choking!

What *had* happened?

While Captain James T. West was trying to understand why he was still alive, his partner, Artemus Gordon, was in an upstairs bedroom, hoping to find a missing scientist or two. But instead he discovered Rita, one of the dancers from the party. She was locked in an iron cage, and she was terrified.

Gordon squinted at her through the shadows and frowned. The woman gasped audibly and opened her mouth to scream. Quickly, Gordon held up his hand to silence her.

"Ma'am, please," he whispered desperately. "While I realize I look pretty strange in this outfit, I mean you no harm. My name is Artemus Gordon, and you look like you're in trouble."

"Oh really?" the woman retorted sarcastically.

But Gordon wasn't listening. He was too busy opening his mountain man jacket and yanking out a tool kit that would make any carpenter proud. As the woman watched in amazement, he pulled out a thin cable and attached it to a tiny wheel on the spur of one of his boots.

"I'm Rita," the woman told him. "I was hired here as an entertainer. Not that I'm complaining, but what are you doin' in here?"

"I was looking for some missing scientists," Gordon explained. "But here you are! Not that *I'm* complaining!"

Gordon unsnapped the sole of his shoe and placed it under his foot, like a pedal.

Next, he removed a bit and handle from his vest and attached it to the thin cable. As he pumped his foot again and again, the wheel on his spur began to turn.

"The Artemus Gordon foot-powered drill!" he announced proudly as the drill buzzed away at the cage lock.

"I'm a special U.S. Marshall on assignment from the President," Gordon explained.

"Well," Rita said sarcastically, "if you're so special, then how come you're lookin' up here when Loveless has all the scientists working down in the dungeon?" She rattled the bars impatiently. "Get me out of here," she pleaded, "and I'll take you down there."

Without looking up from his work, Gordon shook his head. "Too late," he said. "The dungeon is cleaned out. It was the first place I checked, right after I sampled the gumbo, which was, by the way, a bit heavy on the okra."

Finally, the lock clicked and the cage

door swung open. Gordon leaned inside and lifted her out.

Rita's face lit up in a smile. "Thank you, uh, Artemus, wasn't it?"

"One doesn't forget a smile like that," Gordon said. "I've seen you before, but where?"

Outside the window, the crowd was roaring. Gordon suddenly remembered his partner. He knew that West wasn't dead, assuming they tried to hang him with the trick rope he had tossed to them at the party. But he'd better get him out of there before they found another one with a noose that didn't stretch.

Gordon grabbed Rita by the hand and led her down the stairs and out to the stable. Within minutes they were racing a team of horses toward the courtyard, where West was still wondering why he wasn't dead.

With nostrils flaring and eyes wide, the horses burst into the crowd at full speed and headed straight toward West.

Uh-oh! Watch out!

But West was ready. As the team approached, he gave "George Washington" a swift kick, grabbed his gun, and somersaulted into the air . . . straight onto the wagon that was being driven by his partner.

The rope around West's neck began to stretch again. Gordon whirled around, and with his best Bowie knife, he cut the rope, and West was free.

The wagon was speeding through the New Orleans night as West moved forward and whispered in Gordon's ear.

"'Hang him'???? Did I hear you tell them to *hang* me?"

He was about to say a lot more when a volley of shots whizzed past his head. As the others ducked, West used the gun to rid the world of several rebels who were hard on their heels. When he was finished with that little job, he turned back to his partner.

"'*Hang* him'???"

"Meet my trigger-happy partner, James West," Gordon sighed, turning to Rita. "I myself do not like guns at all. I choose to use my intelligence. Mr. West doesn't seem to realize that my *carefully planned* diversion gave me the opportunity to search for the missing scientists."

West took one look at Rita and raised his eyebrows. "Scientists, huh?"

"This is Rita," Gordon explained. "I found her locked in a cage in Loveless's bedroom. She's an entertainer."

"Well," Rita said, slightly embarrassed. "Maybe I haven't been quite honest about that. I came to find Guillermo Escobar, the scientist. He's my father."

Gordon's eyes widened with surprise.

76

"Professor Escobar!" he said. "He was the one I almost rescued that night when . . ."

Suddenly Gordon remembered something. "Wait a minute! Now I know where I've seen you! You sang before I did at Fat-Can Candy's."

"Excuse me?"

"That was me in the burgundy dress with the bustle. Soiled Dove." Gordon opened his mouth and began to sing the song he was singing the night he met West for the first time.

West listened for a minute, then couldn't bear it any longer. "Look, Rita," he said. "I'm sorry you had Gordon, the wrong agent, working on your case. When I find your father I promise I'll send him back safely."

As Rita smiled, West leapt over her and landed on the back of one of the horses. He grabbed a handful of mane, leaned down, and unclipped the harness. Then, with one quick kick, he sent the horse forward and was off at a gallop, leaving his partner and a very surprised Rita in the dust.

CHAPTER 10

Dr. Arliss Loveless held his glass of champagne and toasted the dignitaries who had come together on his boat. He had invited foreign dignitaries from all over the world, for he had something very important to show them. Near the railing, General McGrath stood silent and pensive. Loveless wheeled over and handed him a glass of champagne.

"Well, General," he said. "It's been a long journey from that terrible battle at New Liberty."

McGrath winced and shook his head.

"Sir," he said, "there isn't a day that passes that I don't think about it."

"Yes, and so do I," Loveless agreed, as he thought about his missing legs. "If I'd only had the scientific understanding of gunpowder and primers that I have today."

"That's not what I meant, sir."

For a moment Loveless was confused, but then he remembered. New Liberty, Illinois.

"Oh," he said, "you mean the stomach-churning carnage that earned you your unfortunate *nom de guerre?*"

Loveless turned and faced the dignitaries. "What was that nickname again?" he asked, in a voice loud enough for everyone to hear.

The dignitaries waited politely as McGrath worked up the courage to tell them.

"Bloodbath McGrath," he said softly. "The Butcher of New Liberty."

Beside Loveless, Miss Lippenreider was peering at the shore through a pair of binoculars. From her vantage point in the Gulf of Mexico, she could make out a battalion of rebels on Malheureux Point. The rebels were waiting in a foggy meadow that sloped down to the marsh. As the rebels spoke, she translated.

"They ought to be here by now," the first rebel was saying.

"Maybe we're in the wrong place," another answered.

"No," said a third. "We're supposed to wait 'xactly on this here spot."

Suddenly a clanking and screeching sound caused the rebels to ready their arms and turn toward the sound.

Something was moving toward them. A huge weapon! It was moving up through the mud and the reeds, closer and closer. What was it? It was made of metal and seemed to be as big as a house. A large cannon rose from the top of it, and Gatling guns bristled from several ports.

The rebels let out a cheer that brought smiles to the faces of the dignitaries on Loveless's boat.

The rebels had never seen an armored tank before. No one, in fact, had ever seen an armored tank before.

As the rebels watched, a mortar appeared through the turret and fired a rocket over their heads. The rocket exploded in the air, lighting up the field, bringing into full view the series of rings, like a giant dartboard, that Loveless had designed earlier. Positioned within the rings of the dartboard, they were, it seemed, to be the designated target.

But the rebels, blinded by the bright light, missed it.

Suddenly, as the confused and anxious rebels blinked, the tank turret opened fire on them. Shocked and surprised, the rebels stared straight ahead, then began to fire back with their Springfield rifles.

It was no use. Their bullets pinged off the tank's impenetrable skin and fell to the ground.

On board the boat, McGrath couldn't believe what he had just seen. He flew into a rage as he faced Loveless.

"Why, you sawed-off sadistic maniac!" he shouted. "You've betrayed us! You've mowed down your own men!"

"*My* men?" Loveless hissed. "*My* men? My dear general, after donating half my physical being to creating a weapon capable of doing *this,* how did you and General Lee repay my loyalty? You *surrendered* at Appomattox. You gave up. So, who betrayed whom?"

Miss Lippenreider was interpreting now. "Scream," she was saying. "Scream, scream, my head . . ."

"Loveless!" McGrath cried. "I demand that you give the order to stop this slaughter now!"

"We're going to need more loading drills," Loveless said, ignoring him. "I'm hearing too much time between screams."

"For the last time," McGrath shouted angrily, "give them the order to desist!"

Loveless felt McGrath's gun barrel at his head, but he did not seem to care. "General," he said calmly, "I understand your distress. But believe me, those men are not dying senselessly. It is for a far greater cause than you can imagine."

As he spoke, Loveless moved his right index finger toward the black button on the arm of his wheelchair. With one push of the button, the guns hidden in his armrests would rid the world of the horrible General Bloodbath McGrath.

McGrath's finger tightened on the trigger of his gun. But he was not quick enough. Loveless saw it coming, and pushed the button, leaving McGrath crumpled on the deck.

Dr. Loveless smiled malevolently at his guests. "Well gentlemen," he said politely. "That concludes the festivities."

Then he turned and started to roll off the boat as two of his women dumped McGrath's still body into the Gulf of Mexico.

As the dignitaries followed, Loveless wheeled toward the battlefield and watched his beloved tank move toward the railroad tracks. *What a spectacular sight!* he thought. Look at how it climbs so smoothly onto the rails. And the wheels! What beautiful wheels! The wheels were dropping from the chassis now, and locking into the tracks, and Dr. Loveless was grinning proudly.

"Gentlemen," he said to the awed dignitaries, "if you don't want to miss the ride, have your last payment of one thousand kilograms of your country's gold in my hands no later than Friday. That's when I will make our little proposal to President Grant. One that I am confident he will accept. The South, gentlemen, will indeed rise!"

CHAPTER 11

Later, when the battlefield was deadly quiet and the night was dark, Jim West rode his stallion through the carnage and looked around him. He was alone.

He slid from his horse slowly and shook his head. There was something so familiar about this scene. The mangled bodies. The tread marks in the dirt.

West drew his weapon and walked carefully through the piles of victims. He was looking for something, for someone, who didn't seem to be there.

Eventually Gordon and Rita caught up with him. The horror that surrounded them left Rita feeling sick and Gordon perplexed and confused.

Gordon was thinking out loud. "It came out of the lake, from the way these corpses are positioned. It laid down a 360-degree pattern of cannon fire. A perfect circle of death and destruction. Then it disappeared in moments. My God!" he exclaimed. "What kind of weapon is it?"

"It just rolls on and on," West said, joining them. "It makes a screeching sound, like a wounded animal. It's got a cabin on the top with a cannon in it that swivels round and round like an eagle's head."

"You saw it?" Gordon asked.

"I heard about it. I thought it was just the stories of crazy survivors."

"What survivors?" Gordon asked. "There aren't any survivors here."

"New Liberty, Illinois," West said. "The free slave town just over the border. Just one week before the war ended in 1865. I was in the Ninth Cavalry that discovered it. Old men, women, children. It was a weapon like this one. They used those people for target practice."

As West and Gordon looked over the battlefield, thinking about New Liberty, a moaning sound drifted toward them from the shoreline. They turned and, with Rita behind them, followed the sound. It was coming from the gray washed-up face of General McGrath.

West's eyes narrowed as he studied the man who was responsible for New Liberty. So he wasn't dead — yet.

"What's the matter, West? I thought you'd be happy to find me like this," McGrath moaned.

"I was hoping to kill you myself," West told him.

"You'll have to live with it," McGrath said. "As I've had to live with the blame for New Liberty."

West didn't catch the implication of that one at all. "What's *that* supposed to mean?" he asked.

McGrath's voice was soft and weak as he explained. "It was Loveless. It was his plan. He operated the killing machine there. He's smarter now. He left it to others here."

West shook his head. He had spent so much time hating McGrath that he was reluctant to believe him at first. But he could tell from the dying man's tone that he was telling the truth. Slowly, his hatred shifted from McGrath to Loveless.

"Where is he?" West whispered angrily. "Where did he go?"

McGrath moved his lips, trying to speak, but no words came out. West put his ear closer to the general's mouth, but there were no more words. Finally, McGrath closed his eyes for the last time and died.

West stood and gazed out over the

When U.S. Marshall Artemus Gordon met U.S. Army Captain James West it was dislike at first sight! Would they *ever* be able to team up?

When it came to motoring, West sat high in the saddle of his champion stallion . . .

. . . while Gordon saddled up his, uh, motor-bicycle, the first of its kind.

Dr. Arliss Loveless, the evil genius planning to make sure that the USA—a country once divided—never truly unites.

Gordon shows West his latest invention.
He thinks it will help track
down Dr. Loveless.

Both men got a little "hot under the collar" when Loveless held them captive in a field!

West had to climb atop a tall, treacherous mechanical "tarantula" to rescue President Grant, Gordon, and the entire nation!

Captain James West in yet another sticky situation.

Gordon's invention, the "desert wasp," was the first "flying" machine!

James West—a wild kinda guy
and definitely a winner!

water. He was thinking about Loveless. He would find that monster if it was the last thing he ever did.

Rita tapped him on the shoulder. "I know where Loveless is going," she said gently.

West turned and waited for her to explain.

"I'll tell you if you take me along," she said.

"Just tell me!"

"The girls at the mansion talk. They talk about a place called Ooo-tah."

"Ooo-tah?" West and Gordon said, together. They understood now. Loveless was on his way to Utah. And President Grant was going that way too, to join the tracks for the first trans-American railroad.

Within an hour, West, Gordon, and Rita were aboard the *Wanderer* and heading toward Utah. Rita was devouring the food that Gordon had prepared, and West was watching her. He couldn't believe that anyone could eat that much and that fast. And he wasn't at all happy about her being on that train with them.

"I can help you," Rita said between bites.

"How could you possibly help us?" West asked.

"Well, I heard you talking about why all those foreign guys were at Loveless's party. Do you want me to tell you?"

"By all means," Gordon said.

Rita took another bite and grinned at Gordon. "This food is fantastic!" she exclaimed. "You can cut it with a fork. How'd you cook it?"

"Well," Gordon explained, smiling proudly, "I cooked it in a clay pot. It's a French method which . . ."

"What about the foreign guys?" West impatiently interrupted.

"They were mad about something," Rita

said. "It was something about a bad deal in Louisiana on purpose."

"The Louisiana Purchase?" Gordon asked.

"That's right," Rita replied. "And Queen somebody-somebody of France got swindled."

"Queen Isabella of *Spain*." Gordon understood. Spain had once owned all that land west of the Mississippi River, and had given it to France. Then France sold it to the United States, and perhaps Queen Isabella thought that, somehow, it was rightfully hers.

West was becoming more and more impatient. "Gordon!" he said. "This is crazy! She doesn't know what she's talking about!"

West picked up the speakerphone and called Coleman in the front of the train. "Coleman!" he shouted. "Stop the train! Miss Escobar's getting off."

"We're not putting anybody off!" Coleman shouted back. "Not out here in the middle of nowhere."

West peered through the window. There was nothing out there but sagebrush and animal skulls. Rita moved closer to West, her big brown eyes filled with fear.

"Please, Jim," she begged. "My father's the only family I've got. What am I supposed to do? Should I sit home and wait for news that he's been killed, or go do something? What would you do, Jim?"

"Look, Rita," West said, softening. "I've got nothing against you. But what's going to happen when we catch up to Loveless, with *you* on the train?"

"I assure you, Rita," Gordon said, rising to his feet, "an attack by Loveless would be an exercise in futility. Allow me to demonstrate how my design suggestions for this train have made the *Wanderer* impervious to attack."

Gordon rapped his knuckles against the

wall and grinned smugly at the metallic sound.

"Completely armor-plated," he said.

Then, demonstrating that the light fixture was actually a Gatling gun, he grinned again.

As Rita watched with astonishment, Gordon moved to the pool table and rolled a billiard ball into the bumper.

"And if by some inconceivable fluke they did manage to gain entrance, a billiard ball may appear innocent . . ."

Gordon raised the ball and pressed on the number. ". . . but if you depress the number, this small ball turns into a sleeping gas bomb. They will find that it is effective in under three seconds."

"Speaking of sleeping," Rita yawned, "I'm pretty tired. I think I'll go into that stateroom and get a little sleep."

Gordon and West watched her go. When the stateroom door was tightly closed, they looked at each other and frowned.

"Hey," West said, a moment later, "just when did we say that she could stay?"

"I really don't know, Jim," Gordon smiled. "I really don't know."

CHAPTER 12

The next morning, Gordon and West were sitting in the parlor car when Coleman's voice boomed through the pipe.

"We have Loveless!" he shouted. "He's seven hundred yards ahead of us."

Gordon and West jumped to their feet and scrambled for their boots and weapons.

"What's going on?" Rita asked sleepily as she emerged from her stateroom.

Gordon grabbed her arm quickly and ushered her to the rear of the car. "Stay back here!" he commanded. "And take cover!"

Rita ducked as Gordon made his way back to West, who was struggling to get his boot onto his foot. When he was finally successful, he stood up and glanced down in amazement as a three-inch stiletto snapped out of the toe.

"What the hell is this!" he cried.

"I took the liberty of installing it while you were sleeping," Gordon said proudly.

West turned and glared at him incredulously. "Leave my stuff alone!" he shouted. "Just . . ."

Before he could finish his thought, Coleman's voice interrupted him. "We're closing in," he announced through the pipe.

The *Wanderer* was right behind Loveless's tank/train now, as they moved, in line, into a mountain tunnel. But by the time they emerged, Loveless's machine was nowhere to be seen!

Coleman couldn't believe his eyes. The tracks ahead were definitely empty, but that was impossible.

Or not. It seemed that nothing about

Loveless's new contraption was impossible. One minute Loveless's tank/train had been in front of him, and the next minute it was behind him. But how?

Coleman had missed Loveless's little trick because it had happened inside the dark tunnel. The evil doctor's contraption was equipped with metal stilts that unfolded at the push of a button. And someone on board had obviously pushed that button, for the stilts had emerged. Loveless's train had stopped and raised up on the metal legs, and the *Wanderer* had passed beneath it, oblivious.

When the *Wanderer* was in front, the tank had folded the legs up onto its side, dropped back down onto the tracks, and chased Coleman's pride and joy out of the tunnel.

Gordon noticed that Loveless was *behind,* not *in front of,* the *Wanderer* before West did.

"Jim," he called, as he glanced out the back of the parlor car, "we're the ones chasing Loveless, correct? So perhaps you could explain what he's doing behind us?"

Before West had a chance to explain anything, a shell exploded to the right of their train . . . *ka-boom!* Then another, to the left . . . *ka-boom!* Then another, and another, and another. *Ka-boom! Ka-boom! Ka-boom!*

As Gordon, West, and Rita flew back and forth on the rocking train, West said, "They're behind us because they couldn't fire the cannon at us if they were in front. Any other questions?"

West jumped up onto the pool table and looked down at Gordon. It was time to pay Dr. Loveless a visit, and an upside-down pool table was the quickest way out.

"Would it put you out too much to throw me a rope and hit your secret button?"

Gordon shrugged and tossed West a rope. Then he leaned over and pushed the secret button on the pool table, causing it to flip over. In a second, West was hanging upside down under the *Wanderer*. Hand over hand, West moved beneath the train until he reached the small escape trolley that was hanging there. The trolley was the size of a little red wagon, with wheels that fit perfectly in the tracks below.

Carefully, he slid himself onto the trolley and lowered it onto the track, making sure that its wheels were firmly locked in.

He was ready now. With a quick *click,* he released the cable and shot backward on the trolley, dodging bullets, toward the tank/train behind him.

Inside the train, Gordon opened a panel in the floor and began to crank a large handle, letting out the cable that was attached to the trolley. With each turn of the handle,

West moved further and further from the *Wanderer* and closer and closer to Loveless's train.

What was this! Something was clearly wrong. The trolley, with West on it, was jerking now. Something was wrong with the cable that connected the trolley to the *Wanderer*. It was yanking back and forth. And then, suddenly, the trolley was flying out of control. The cable had snapped, and the trolley had broken loose.

It was moving now, faster and faster, toward the tank/train behind them.

A Gordon invention had failed again.

West flew backward at an incredible speed, and just as it seemed that his head would be removed by Loveless's tank/train contraption, he slid beneath it and watched as it roared past above him.

Watch out! That was a close one! Next?

West spun Gordon's rope in a neat circle and lassoed the rear axle of the tank.

The trolley slowed for a second. But then, for some inexplicable reason, it sped up again, sending him backward again and scaring him half to death.

Gordon, it seemed, had given him one of his trick ropes, and it had stretched. *Stretched.* What the . . . !

"Artemus!" West screamed as he bolted backward, then sprang forward toward Loveless's train. "Hello! Hello! Anybody there? Yo?" But no one heard him, of course, above the roar of the tank and the screech of the wheels.

West zoomed toward the tank/train and grabbed hold of the back. He swung his legs up and pulled himself onto the step and then up onto the roof. Thinking. Mind racing. Gotta get to the smokestack! Gotta get that flue closed! Close that flue and before ya know it the tank'll be filled with smoke, and Loveless will be coughing so hard he won't even be able to *see* the *Wanderer,* let alone shoot at it. Yup, that's the trick! That should do it!

But one of Loveless's men was too fast for him. Coming up from behind, he had West by the throat. That's it then, Jim thought. But then he remembered his boot. Would Gordon's invention work this time? It had to. He clicked his heels and watched . . . Whew! The stiletto blade shot out!

With one swift kick of the blade, he removed his pursuer, kicking him into the smokestack and handily plugging up the flue.

Below, Loveless's train was filling with smoke. As West had hoped, Loveless and the others began to choke. They coughed and sputtered. And then, just as Loveless ordered the fire door shut, the boiler exploded and the back of the tank/train blew up. It jerked. It rattled.

The *Wanderer* would have been out of harm's way, except for one thing. When

West abandoned the trolley, the little wagon had shot forward and Gordon had caught the rope and tied it to his train. The two trains were connected by the trolley and a rope that could only stretch so far. And when Loveless's train exploded, and crashed to a stop, the trick rope stretched then yanked the beautiful *Wanderer* backward into the tank/train, stopping it in its tracks.

Rita was terrified! What if Loveless captured her once again? That, plus the fear of being alone, propelled her into action.

With one hand she grabbed a sleeping-gas pool ball, and with the other she clutched a confused Gordon. She yanked him into a stateroom and locked the door, hoping that the lock would protect her.

Gordon and Rita sat on the bed and waited for a few minutes. Then they heard the approaching footsteps. The door handle jiggled.

Gordon gestured to Rita to be still. Rita nodded, and raised the pool ball. Loveless would not take *her*. She was ready.

A smoke-hoarse voice called out from the other side of the door. "It's me, Jim," the strange voice said. "Open up."

But Rita didn't believe it. In fact, she was so sure it was a trick — that it was Loveless on the other side of the door, pretending to be Jim — that she pushed the number on the ball before Gordon could stop her. The ball dropped to the floor at the exact moment West, huffing and puffing, managed to get the stateroom door open. Assuming he was safe, he grinned that satisfied grin of his . . .

. . . until he saw the pool ball rolling between his feet, spewing a purple cloud of sleeping gas.

Captain James T. West was not having a good day!

CHAPTER 13

When West opened his eyes, he wasn't anywhere that he had ever been before. He was lying on the ground, surrounded by high corn stalks. He raised his head, turned, recognized a familiar face, and groaned.

"An innocent billiard ball this way . . . ," he said, mimicking Gordon, who was slowly waking up beside him. ". . . but if you depress the number, it becomes, on impact, a sleeping-gas bomb!"

West shook his head and glared at Gordon. Then he pulled himself to his feet and examined the metal band around his neck with his fingers. Someone must have placed it there while he was sleeping. That, *and* the circle of wire fence that now surrounded the two of them.

West approached the fence and started to step over it.

"Don't move!" Gordon shouted, grabbing his leg.

"Let go of my leg!" West shouted back.

But Gordon hung on. "Listen," he said, "Loveless collared both of us with the same metal device we found on the headless Dr. Morton. You do remember him, don't you?"

How could West forget that unfortunate scientist? He was shaking his leg violently, trying to free himself, when he noticed Loveless watching them from the *Wanderer*. He shook his head to clear it, then suddenly realized that Rita wasn't with them.

"What have you done with Rita?" Jim called to Loveless.

"Rita, is it?" Loveless called back, taunting. "How familiar! Your friend Rita is sleeping off the aftereffects in the stateroom. Quite lovely, isn't she? But now it is time to move on, gentlemen. You don't mind if I borrow your marvelous train, do you? I find it a most comfortable way to pass the long miles from here to my laboratory in Spider Canyon."

Loveless was overseeing the loading of the two thirty-six-inch-round metal discs into a metal contraption. It was the same contraption that he had used to decapitate the unlucky Dr. Morton. When he was finished, he ordered the train to move out. As it chugged away, Loveless began to giggle hysterically. The giggle grew louder and louder, echoing across the field. Abruptly, it ceased in mid-giggle, as Loveless shouted, "I'll be seeing President Grant soon at Promontory Point. What should I tell him for you? I'm afraid it *can't* be that you're alive and well."

West yanked at the metal collar. "Gordon," he spat angrily. "Get out your little tool kit and get this thing off of me!"

Gordon stood, unbuttoned his shirt, and pulled out his leather kit. But when he opened it, he found that it was empty, except for a note in an unfamiliar handwriting, probably Loveless's.

"'Gentlemen,'" Gordon read, "'Welcome to the Loveless Experimental Camp for Political Dissidents. There are no guards in this camp. There is no barbed wire. As long as you stay within the designated perimeter, you will remain alive.'"

"How do you know it's true?" West challenged.

"You can step over the fence and find out," Gordon suggested. "Rita and I will put flowers on your grave every year."

West moved closer to the little fence and studied it. "I don't have time for this," he said, exasperated.

Gordon leaned over and peeled back the toe of his boot. He always kept a spare tool kit in there, and Loveless hadn't discovered it. He was about to pull it out, when Jim jumped over the fence.

"You see," West said. "Nothing happened."

Before Gordon had a chance to answer, his partner leaned over, grabbed him by the back of his vest, and yanked him over the fence. Gordon wasn't prepared for this turn of events. Not by any means. And he certainly was not prepared for the buzzing sound that suddenly reverberated somewhere near his head.

The metal disc whizzed past him toward West, but at the last possible second West ducked and the disc continued on, severing the tops of the stalks.

"Oh really?" Gordon said sarcastically. "So nothing happened, did it?"

They were both outside the perimeter

of the fence now, and running like crazy, running for their lives, through the cornfield.

They zigged! They zagged! They ducked! They dove! The steady stream of magnetic metal discs that were flying past, trying their best to connect with the heavy round magnetic collars couldn't get these guys! Not with all that jumping and leaping and twirling about!

Inside the *Wanderer*, Rita was finally waking from the effects of the billiard ball gas. As she opened her eyes, she was sickened to see Loveless on the other side of the room.

"Rita, my dear," he gushed. "Not that I'm ungrateful to the powers that be for bringing you back to me. It's just that I'm a wee bit curious as to how you managed to wind up with *them*."

"Well, uh, they . . ." Rita was nervously scrambling for words. "They seemed so sure that they could find you, and I thought if I stayed with them, they'd lead me back to . . . all my friends."

Loveless appeared unconvinced.

"And not to give you a big head, or anything, but . . . I kinda missed you," Rita added.

Clearly, Loveless didn't believe her at all. "Isn't that a coincidence?" he said sarcastically, referring to his missing legs. "I miss me too."

As the train moved down the track, the metal discs exploded from it like giant razors, zooming across the cornfield, mowing down stalks, searching for the magnetic collars around the necks of the marked men, West and Gordon.

Racing through the corn, West and Gordon sidestepped, and, somehow, against all odds, emerged alive.

"Head for that cliff!" Gordon shouted as they ran toward the last of the cornstalks.

They raced toward the rocks, slid to a stop, looked down, and gasped. Below them, for 100 feet, was nothing but air, dropping into a feeble ribbon of brown water.

A disc buzzed over their heads. Then another, and another, as they leapt to the left, and the right, and . . .

"When I give the signal, jump off the cliff into my arms!" West shouted.

"Are you crazy?" Gordon shouted back. "Do you see what's down there?"

The discs were coming every second now. There was only one thing left to do.

"Five, four, three, two . . ." West shouted as he held out his arms.

"Forget it!" Gordon hollered. "I'm not doing it!"

"ONE!" West hollered back as he leapt into the air and dropped down through the canyon.

Gordon followed, his eyes closed in terror, and when he was halfway down, flying toward the brown river, he opened them and gazed into the eyes of his partner.

"I just remembered," he whispered, terrified. "I can't swim!"

CHAPTER 14

*T*HUK! THUK!

The sounds of West and Gordon hitting the brown riverbed echoed through the deep canyon. In a way, Gordon was relieved, because there wasn't enough water to drown him. But the mud that covered all but his head wasn't much better. He looked around and found his partner, groaning beside him, trying to extract himself from the brown gook.

When they were finally free, they moved slowly into the desert, dragging their poor bruised, tattered bodies through the sage-brush.

West saw the big fat poisonous lizard first. He knew what it was — a Gila monster — and he knew if he could catch it, they'd have the perfect dinner. Correction: the *only* dinner they could hope for, under the circumstance. He did not have to chase it far, for the animal seemed even more tired than he was, and when he caught it he brought it back to Gordon.

They made a fire. While the Gila monster was cooking, Gordon worked on the collar around West's neck until it was free. Then he handed his tools to West so he could do the same.

West grabbed the sizzling Gila monster and ripped it apart. He handed some to Gordon, then began to devour his part. He was so busy chomping and slurping at the delicious meat that he did not notice Gordon staring at him, appalled.

"What?!" he said, annoyed, when he finally did. "Are my manners upsetting your gentlemanly sensibilities?"

Gordon raised his eyes to the heavens and began to recite something from Shakespeare, rambling on and on until, finally, he happened to notice that West was glaring at him.

"What?!" he demanded.

"You know, Gordon, you can be quite annoying — flaunting that fancy education of yours."

"Well," Gordon admitted sheepishly, "truth be told, I never had a fancy education. Not a formal one, anyway."

West glanced down at Gordon's Harvard class ring. "That Harvard thing seems pretty formal to me."

"This ring? This ring isn't real. Do you want it?" Gordon yanked off the ring and tossed it into the fire. "It's a prop," he explained. "I'm an actor, or at least I was. I gave it up. My stage name was Arthur Gordon. Ever heard of me?"

West shook his head. "How did you wind up in this line of work?" he asked between bites.

Gordon felt relieved. It was time to tell West — his partner — his story.

He began.

"The pinnacle of my life in the theater came in a production of *Our American Cousin.* It was a light comedy at the Ford's Theater in Washington, D.C. There was this one line I had, and it always got the biggest laugh in the show. One night, the date was April 14, 1865, I was reciting this line and I was drowned out by the sound of the gunshot that killed President Lincoln. His murderer, John Wilkes Booth, leapt from the presidential box, only to be captured and killed twelve days later. I, on the other hand, decided to devote my talents to making sure that never happened again."

Gordon glanced down at West's hand and hesitated. A huge tarantula was strolling across his partner's palm.

"Uh, there's a spider on your hand," Gordon said. "Doesn't that bother you?"

West barely noticed the large hairy creature. He was thinking about Gordon's story. He wanted to say something — that he understood, or was sorry.

"This spider doesn't want any trouble," West explained after a moment. "She's just trying to get warm. People think that tarantulas are dangerous, but they're not. Like many creatures, it looks scarier than it really is."

"How come you know so much about the desert?" Gordon asked.

"The Indians taught me. I lived out here when I was a boy. They taught me to survive. One was a healer. He was my friend. He said that he could change into a bird and if I ever needed him he would fly to my side."

West pointed toward a small black wasp that was flying over Gordon's head.

"Watch out for that little thing," he said. "The desert wasp is one of the world's great hunters. She'll kill a tarantula, and lay her eggs on it so that the babies can have something to eat when they hatch."

Gordon took this in, then asked, "So, how did your parents, who I assume were black, feel about you being raised by Indians?"

"They didn't have much to say about it. I was sent to another plantation when I was little. They took me from my family. I ran away as soon as my legs were strong enough to take me."

Gordon watched his partner, his eyes filled with sympathy.

"Did you ever see your family again?" he asked.

West stood then, and kicked out the fire angrily. "I saw them," he said. "They were at the camp at New Liberty, wiped out, with the others, by our friend Dr. Loveless."

"I'll help you get him, Jim," Gordon promised softly.

They slept side by side in the desert, and the next morning they trudged through endless sand dunes together. Finally they were partners, real partners.

"You have no idea where you're going, do you?" Gordon huffed as they climbed over what seemed like sand dune number 1,000. It was late the following morning and they were on their way to . . . somewhere.

"I know exactly where I'm going," West assured him. "I'm going to Spider Canyon. But I'm never going to get there with you draggin' that thing around."

West pointed to the heavy metal collar that Gordon was lugging behind him.

"While a magnet of this power may not inspire your scientific curiosity," Gordon explained, "it does mine. Besides, you never know when it might come in handy."

West groaned and rolled his eyes heavenward. This guy was seriously nuts. After a while he turned, but Gordon wasn't there. One minute he had been beside him and the next minute he was just . . . gone. And then he saw him, lying on his back, the magnetic metal collar held straight up in the air over his head. Gordon was being dragged backward across the desert floor by some unseen force!

The force was pulling him faster, then faster still, until he came to a crashing halt against some iron railroad tracks that had been hidden by drifting sand.

"Artemus," West laughed, unrolling his eyes. "You have found the tracks that will lead us to our destination. When you're right, you're right."

"Well, I think our partnership is taking a big step forward," Gordon said, chagrined. "You finally admitted I was right about something."

West helped his partner up and, together, they followed the train tracks toward Spider Canyon.

CHAPTER 15

Gordon could not believe his eyes. For a moment he thought he was seeing a mirage, for there, sitting on the tracks, was his beloved train, the *Wanderer*. And better yet, it appeared to be deserted, except for the horses that were tied to the back. He and West stopped for a moment to examine it, then moved on to Spider Canyon and peered over the rim. The sight at the bottom of the canyon was even more astonishing than the sight of the *Wanderer*.

The canyon spread out below them was like a giant bowl, filled with several spectacular glass buildings and a huge silo. People were moving around the bowl, doing something that Gordon could not figure out.

"That," West explained, "is the lair of Dr. Arliss Loveless."

"So it is," Gordon agreed. "But what, may I ask, is that strange sound?"

Neither of them had ever heard a sound like it before. As they tried to identify it, the whining, buzzing *whir* grew louder, and then, suddenly, a steel platform loomed up before them, rising out of the bowl. And riding on the platform elevator, approaching them from the canyon, was a multileveled metal contraption taller than any they'd ever seen before.

West and Gordon turned and scrambled for cover behind a rock, then peeked out and waited. What *was* this thing?

As the contraption rose up to the level of the canyon rim, an enormous metal tarantula, five stories high with eight giant legs, stepped off and moved toward them. The thorax of the iron spider bristled with Gatling guns and other weapons that Gordon and West had never seen before.

"Now *that's* impressive," Gordon said reverentially as the shadow of the monster passed over their faces.

"It's nice to see an invention that works," West agreed sarcastically. "And isn't that Loveless in the driver's seat?"

Indeed it was. As they gazed at this dazzling sight, Loveless and his crew steered the tarantula toward a narrow opening between two outcroppings of rock. Loveless was beaming. He was on top of the world.

"We'll see about that!" Gordon clucked as he studied the too-small opening. "That thing can't make it between those rocks. The fool doesn't even realize he's trapped!"

Whoa! Was there nothing this giant spider couldn't do! A volley of cannon fire reduced the rocks to dust and the tarantula marched on easily.

West and Gordon raced to the safety of the *Wanderer*. West scrambled through the train, getting ready. Within minutes, he was dressed for battle. His six-shooters were strapped onto his hips. His coach gun was tucked behind his chaps. His shotgun-shell bandolero was belted around his waist. More guns were placed here and there on other parts of his body. Captain James T. West was definitely prepared for war.

"Gordon," he exclaimed as he stuck his head out the door. "Let's ride! You do know how to ride, don't you?"

Gordon had discovered his Nitro-Cycle on the train, and he was busy fiddling with it. He was doing something with a piece of canvas that West couldn't figure out.

"I meant a horse," West groaned.

"Yes, I know how to ride a horse, when the situation calls for something primitive."

"How about now? There's a big spider stompin' toward our President!"

128

But Gordon was in no mood to be to be hurried. He was studying a big book and his Nitro-Cycle, and he wasn't finished yet.

"I was just thinking about another spider," he mumbled as he peered at his book. "Remember, in the desert, when that little wasp killed the tarantula?"

West was getting exasperated. "Yeah," he sighed. "Well, the wasp had a small advantage. It could fly!"

"Exactly!"

Gordon shoved the book in front of his partner and pointed to a diagram of a weird aircraft.

"At the end of the fifteenth century, Leonardo da Vinci, the noted artist who gave us the *Mona Lisa* and the *Last Supper,* invented a flying machine called the 'Ornithopter.' He drew a diagram of it in his notebook in mirror script, which was extremely difficult to read, and though he never actually completed the project — he often left things unfinished — well, the machine never did get off the ground, of course . . ."

"Artemus!" West interrupted. "There's no time for plans or half-cocked inventions! They don't work! Birds fly. Bugs fly. People do not fly! Now, we gotta stick to what we're good at! We've got to dress you up and fool Loveless into thinking you're somebody else."

West took Gordon by the arm and dragged him to the wardrobe. When Gordon was dressed and ready, West helped him onto a horse and they galloped through the desert toward Promontory Point, Utah.

They were friends. They were partners. Captain James T. West and Artemus Gordon — cleverly disguised as President Ulysses S. Grant!— riding along, side by side, together.

CHAPTER 16

The real President Grant was busy with a ceremony. In a moment he would knock in the spike that would complete the trans-American railroad. Two train engines faced each other, waiting for the final spike to be inserted deep into the ground so that they could continue their journeys all the way across America from west to east and from east to west.

President Grant raised his sledgehammer. The crowd moved closer. They looked down at the spike.

Something was wrong. The spike was trembling. It was wiggling and shaking and

131

then, for no apparent reason, it popped right out of its hole.

President Grant put down the sledgehammer and studied the desert around him.

And then he saw it. The crowd saw it too, and started to scream.

The giant metal Tarantula was walking toward them, quickly, its huge legs covering the distance between them in no time at all. That was what had made the ground shake.

The crowd fluttered and fled. The soldiers surrounding the President took cover and drew their weapons.

But President Grant did not move. He stood firmly and waited as the gigantic creature stopped before him.

The voice of Dr. Loveless boomed through the desert morning.

"Well, isn't this a coincidence! I'm out for a little mornin' ride, and right in the middle of nowhere I bump into General Ulysses S. Grant himself!"

Loveless threw the President a mocking salute and continued.

"We've never been properly introduced. I'm Dr. Arliss Loveless, formerly with the Confederate Army."

Incredible! President Grant didn't seem to be bothered. Calmly, he lit a cigar and grinned.

"Yes, Dr. Loveless. What can I do for you today?"

The President turned toward his military aides and instructed them to flank Dr. Loveless and his strange contraption.

"I have a humble abode nearby," Loveless continued. "And I hope you'll accept my hospitality. I have a little proposition to make."

"What proposition is that?" Grant asked in a mock-bored tone.

Loveless glared down from his perch. "The unconditional and immediate surrender of the United States of America to the Loveless Alliance," he announced.

"I didn't know we were at war," Grant replied calmly.

Suddenly a shot from Loveless's cannon blew the President's train to smithereens, and Loveless began to giggle.

"How about now?" he asked.

The terrified crowd scattered. One, however, did not run away. Calmly, he strolled to the burning train and used the flames to light his cigar. Then he joined the President and shouted up at Loveless, "In matters of war, the person to talk to would be me!"

What was this? Who was this? Loveless couldn't believe his eyes. The person standing below him looked exactly like President Grant. But how could that be? Because the other person standing below him also looked exactly like President Grant.

And he wasn't the only one surprised by this turn of events. The real President Grant was amazed.

"Now just who are you?" Loveless asked.

"The President," Gordon informed him. He turned, pointed to the real President, and snorted. "He's just an actor hired to stand in for me on public occasions. A very bad actor, I must say. A little puffy and overweight."

President Grant groaned. "Gordon," he whispered, so that Loveless couldn't hear him. "You've got a lot of brass. Where's West?"

"You know him, sir . . ."

Grant shifted his gaze to the tarantula, where West was running, unnoticed, toward the rear leg. As the lone cowboy started to climb up toward the belly of the beast, Gordon turned to an Army officer and pointed toward the real President.

"Captain," he ordered, "get this man out of my sight! And next time find me a real actor!"

The bewildered captain nodded and

135

started to lead the President away, but Loveless stopped him. He had had enough.

"Take them both!!!" he shouted.

Munitia, Loveless's most trusted officer, focused the cannon on the two Grants. She pulled the trigger. And as the astonished crowd looked on, both Presidents were engulfed by a sticky white silk spider web material.

"Well, Gordon," the real President Grant said. "Was this part of your plan?"

"I'm by your side, sir," Gordon assured him. "That's what's important."

As they stood there together, two spiders in one web, Munitia hit a lever and they were hoisted up off the ground, a few inches, a few inches more, until . . .

BLAM!

A shot rang out from the lowest deck of the tarantula, short-circuiting the mechanism and jerking it to a stop.

Loveless's goons turned their guns and

focused them toward the lower deck, where West was standing, guns in hand.

West slipped behind a steel girder and began to shoot. All his guns were blazing now. Bullets were flying from the guns of Grant's soldiers too, pinging harmlessly off the tarantula's alloy skin.

Loveless was growing bored.

Yawning, he leaned over and pulled a lever, opening nozzles on the tarantula's legs and engulfing West in clouds of skin-scalding steam.

West screamed. He hollered. He shouted in pain. And then he fell, thirty feet, to the ground below, hitting his head on a rock as he landed.

He lay there for a long time, his body motionless. A line of ants marched slowly across his face, swarming around the bloody cut on the side of his head.

Soon a vulture found him and circled above his silent body, swooping lower, then lower still, until it was on his head and leaning into his face, examining his lifeless eyes.

The red beak moved closer to the eyes, close enough to peck them out — except this bird did not peck. Instead, magically a human hand appeared and brushed the ants away, gently, and West's eyes fluttered open.

He looked up and saw, not a vulture, but the soft face of his Indian friend, the healer who could change into a bird.

West sat up groggily and touched the cut on his head. He was going to be all right.

CHAPTER 17

While West was tending to his wound, Dr. Loveless was addressing the group of foreign dignitaries seated in his amphitheater. As he spoke, everyone applauded . . . everyone, that is, but the haggard scientists and manacled prisoners gathered together on the side. While West had been falling through the abyss, Loveless had gathered President Grant, Rita, Coleman, and Gordon, out of disguise now, together and handcuffed them. And now here they were, forced to listen to this maniac.

"Good day, gentlemen!" he was saying.

"Great, glorious day! A day of healing for the wrongs that have been done to us all!"

As the crowd applauded, Loveless turned to an English dignitary.

"Seventeen seventy-six, wasn't it, that the Declaration of Independence was signed and the U.S.A. tossed you aside. And three years earlier, the Boston Tea Party, some party that was. Dumped all your tea into Boston Harbor? Most expensive cup of tea in history?"

As the English dignitary nodded solemnly, Loveless turned to his favorite Indian.

"And you, Hudson," he said. "How do you feel about the island of Manhattan being taken away from your people in 1626, by the Dutch, perhaps, but still . . . for a measly twenty-four dollars?"

Hudson shook his head in frustration as Loveless addressed the Mexican contingent.

"And you, sir. 'Remember the Alamo' indeed! A battle, sir, just one of the many in the

Mexican–American War in which you lost the state of Texas. What was the year? 1836?"

Loveless looked down at all the dignitaries.

"Today I am proud to be able to sit before you and tell you that all the wrongs will be righted. The past will be made the present. The United States will be . . ." He paused for effect, then pronounced the key word, slowly. "Divided!" he said.

And the crowd cheered. They stamped their feet and called his name as a large map of "The De-United States" appeared behind him.

"The thirteen original colonies, with the exception of Manhattan, will be returned to Great Britain. Florida and the Fountain of Youth go back to Spain. Texas, New Mexico, California, and Arizona will belong to Mexico again. And the Louisiana Purchase reverts back to the King of France!"

Loveless moved closer to the map and tapped Colorado, Kansas, Utah, and Nevada with his pointer. The words "Loveless Land" were printed on them in big letters.

"And a tiny piece for me to retire on," he explained as the dignitaries laughed in appreciation.

Loveless moved to a desk and unrolled a document. Then he signaled for President Grant to be brought forward.

"Never will I sign that paper!" Grant exclaimed as Loveless tried to shove a pen into his clenched hand. "Never will the United States surrender!"

"Well, sir," Loveless said. "I suppose the threat of death to someone with your valorous war record would mean nothing. So, if you still refuse to sign, we'll start by shooting your man Gordon."

Instantly, Gordon was dragged forward and the President was returned to his seat.

"Artemus!" Rita cried.

But Artemus was brave, especially because, as he whispered to Grant and Rita, he was wearing his Impermeable vest.

He turned to Loveless.

"If I may have one request," he said sweetly, "it's that your woman Munitia aim at my heart, which has loved this great country so much!"

"Shoot him in the head!" Loveless ordered.

Munitia cocked her rifle. But then, just as Loveless was about to give the signal to fire, the lights dimmed and a candle-powered spotlight swung across the stage and illuminated a beautiful woman of color clothed in a tight blue sequined dress, black mesh stockings, and a big feather boa.

The woman began to sing, and as she sang . . .

"Ohhhhh . . . Hangtown gals are plump and rosy . . ."

Distracted, Loveless seemed to forget

about Gordon's execution. He couldn't take his eyes off her. She was exquisite!

"Hair in ringlets, mighty cozy!" the woman crooned in a sexy, bluesy voice.

"A new girl!" Loveless gushed. "What a nice surprise! Ebonia!"

Loveless had made up the name on the spot.

As Gordon watched this display, thankful for his reprieve, a little light was beginning to flicker in his memory. There was something odd about all this.

And then it came to him. He had a dress just like that one.

Ebonia was sashaying around the stage, pulling the French dignitary's monocle out of his eye, placing her cheek against the face of the disgusted Rita, and picking the pocket of Loveless's favorite lip reader.

Then, without missing a beat, she handed Coleman the handcuff keys that she had just taken from Miss Lippenreider and pranced toward Gordon.

Coleman and Gordon both understood now. This was no blues singer. This was the crazy captain, James T. West.

"Not to sound ungrateful," Gordon whispered, "but you're a little over the top."

West wrapped the feather boa around Gordon's neck, and as he did so, he passed his partner a derringer. Gordon wasn't sure he wanted a gun. What was he going to do with a gun? He hated guns! But he tucked it up his sleeve anyway.

"Let me warn you about that dress," he whispered to West.

But West wasn't listening. It was time for his big finish. He took a breath! He opened his mouth! He belted it out! The crowd cheered. They roared. They stomped their feet. They were so engrossed that they never even noticed Coleman turn quickly to Grant and Rita and unlock their handcuffs.

"Where'd those keys come from?" Grant whispered.

Coleman nodded toward Ebonia. "Captain West," he whispered back as they gaped, eyes wide, mouths open in amazement.

West was into it now. "One more time!" he shouted, carrying on, spinning the tassels on the front of his dress, faster and faster, noticing finally that there was something very strange about those tassels. As he stopped, they kept going, spinning and spinning, then turning into flamethrowers, exploding and, as he turned, incinerating one of Loveless's henchmen.

As he fell, Rita grabbed the keys from his pocket. She would need them later, to unlock the scientists and set them free. "Kill that person!" Loveless ordered, pointing toward West/Ebonia. The rest of the goons rushed forward, too many of them now, overwhelming West, almost but not quite. Suddenly he remembered something and he reached down into his fancy petticoats and retrieved one of Gordon's billiard balls. He pushed the number and rolled it at the guards as Gordon tried to stop him.

He wasn't in time.

"Was that the eight ball?" Gordon asked West.

"Mmm-hmm."

Gordon grabbed West and Rita and pulled them backward.

"That one's an incendiary bomb," he informed them — just before it exploded. *KA-BOOM!* And the place erupted in flames.

Rita jumped up and raced through the smoke as West and Gordon tried to call her back. But it was no use. She made her way through the fiery amphitheater to a bearded scientist and unlocked his collar. When he was free, she turned to him and smiled.

Coleman was shooting at the goons now — and he had a huge surprise for West and Gordon. He was, he explained, really Special Marshall Coleman, guarding them throughout at the orders of President Grant. And the President himself was shooting now too, until, suddenly, he was tapped from behind, knocked out cold, and carried into the night.

The amphitheater was engulfed by flames and the foreign dignitaries were frantic. But Loveless was blind to them. Still, they called his name, reminding him of their partnership. He fled behind a steel vault door to safety, surrounded by his women and the unconscious President Grant.

A few minutes later, as West, Gordon, and Coleman coughed and gasped their way out of the amphitheater, the tarantula appeared, strutting upward. As they watched helplessly, it moved past them, with the President of the United States held hostage on the bridge.

CHAPTER 18

"C'mon!" Gordon gasped. "We gotta go! We gotta ride a horse! Something!"

"No, Art," West said calmly as he watched the tarantula lumber over the desert and disappear. "We need a plan. That flying machine idea of yours . . . were you just acting like you knew what you were talking about, or could you build it?"

Gordon wasn't sure, but he was willing to try. He would need some materials, and that would take time, but he knew just where they were — on the *Wanderer*. Finally he was ready. At their feet lay a twenty-foot-long expanse of canvas . . . the wing.

"Now," Gordon explained to West and Coleman, "according to Bernoulli's Theorem, a bird's wing is designed so that the air flowing over it is moving faster than the air flowing under it. This means that the air above the wing is moving at a lower pressure than the pressure below the wing. That's called 'lift,' and that's why the bird can stay up in the air. Of course, it's only a theory. No human has ever tested it. No one's ever flown before."

Gordon drew a picture of a wing cutting through the air, showing airflow with arrows and circular lines indicating "lift." When he was finished, he realized that it was upside down, and as he turned it downside-up, he noticed that West was watching him nervously through his goggles. West had found leather flight jackets in the *Wanderer,* and they were both wearing them now.

"You're not makin' me feel any better," West groaned.

Gordon and West attached the wing to the frame and hooked it onto the Nitro-Cycle as Coleman prepared the bombs and handed them to West.

When they were ready, Gordon adjusted his goggles as West climbed onto the contraption behind him. Coleman gave them a farewell wave, and they were off, racing across the desert, building up ground speed.

"*Avant . . . !*" West shouted. "*Avant! . . .*"

But they were not going fast enough. "We're not getting enough lift!" Gordon hollered. "We need more speed!"

Before West had a chance to answer, Gordon spun the machine around and headed straight toward the cliff.

"Hey!" West shouted. "That's a cliff over there, you know!!!"

But Gordon wasn't interested. He was too busy gunning the accelerator, faster and faster, as they shot toward the cliff, and then

beyond it, down, down, and then, suddenly . . .

The Nitro-Cycle swooped up and . . .

They were flying!

"It worked!" Gordon cried, amazed. "It
WORKED!!"

"Well, if you had to get one right," West
called, staring down at the great abyss below,
"I'm real glad it was this one!"

"Yeee . . . haaa!" Gordon hollered, sound-
ing an awful lot like his partner.

And with that, he banked his new invention — sort of a Desert Wasp — around
and flew off to save the Republic.

At that moment, the President of the
Republic — Ulysses Grant — was seated in
front of Loveless on the deck of the tarantula. The mighty spider was heading into a
small town and sending its citizens scattering.

"Mr. President," Loveless was saying. "I'll

ask you once again. Sign the surrender or I will decimate this town."

"You've had my answer," the President said firmly.

"Commence firing!" Loveless ordered.

And with that, the tarantula opened fire.

Gordon and West were directly above the town when the firing commenced, but they were so deep in thought they didn't realize what was happening.

Gordon was musing. "I think I'll call it . . ."

"Lemme guess," West said. "An Elevation Enhancer?"

Gordon glanced over his shoulder at West and wondered if his partner was crazy. Why would he call it something silly like that?

"No, Air . . . Gordon!"

Suddenly West noticed the tarantula and the chaos below.

154

"Go down!" he shouted, pointing. "Down there!"

"You can't just 'go down there,' " Gordon explained, as if to a child. "Flight depends on lift, which must be calibrated to the angle of descent."

"Shut up and go down there, will ya!?"

West reached over and shoved the makeshift joystick forward, sending the Wasp straight down toward the bridge of the tarantula. Gordon pushed him away and strained to keep control.

Below, the evil Dr. Loveless was doing his best to convince President Grant to sign.

"Well, Mr. President," he was saying. "Have you had enough yet? Would you like to sign the surrender, or shall we set a course for Denver? Wichita? Or perhaps we should blow Washington to bits?"

The President was considering his options when a loud whooshing sound broke the mood.

155

West and Gordon swooped down low as the President and everyone else on the tarantula gazed up in amazement.

"Well, I'll be," the President gasped. "It's West and Gordon, flying!"

Loveless had had enough of President Grant. He turned toward Munitia and ordered her to do away with him.

Above, West unfastened bombs from his vest and waited for the right moment. Then, as they swung past the tarantula cannon, he dropped them,

BOOM! BOOM!

And the tarantula's big gun fell limp.

Loveless recoiled, then ordered Munitia to shoot the thing down. But how? He had never counted on having to shoot upwards. No one had ever thought of that, and so, of course, they were unable to raise their weapons higher than 90 degrees.

It took a moment for Loveless to formulate a plan, but when he did, it was a good one. Pushing a lever, he sent the tarantula down on its front knees, and with its rear in the air, he pointed his guns straight up.

Bullets perforated the Desert Wasp's wings and blasted it out of the sky.

"What does your friend da Vinci say about puttin' this bird down?" West shouted as they plummeted toward the earth.

"I don't think he thought it would ever work," Gordon shouted back. "So he didn't get that far. Anyway, he wasn't so good at finishing things."

Munitia was just about to pull the trigger on the gun that would kill the President when West and Gordon landed. The Desert Wasp, alias Air Gordon, crashed into Munitia's back, sending her off the deck.

CHAPTER 19

West and Gordon emerged from the Desert Wasp alive and pretty much intact. Together, they picked up the President and dusted him off.

"Sorry about that, sir," Gordon said. "Nose up, flaps down. I'll have to remember that next time."

"Son," the President said warmly, "never apologize for saving a President's life."

Gordon thought about the night that President Lincoln was shot at the Ford's Theater and felt a little better. Perhaps he had made amends, at last, for the presidential life he had been unable to save that fateful night.

But his thoughts were interrupted as he turned, along with West and Grant, to see Loveless' female goons Amazonia and Lippenreider with guns pointed straight at them.

"Gentlemen," Loveless said, rolling up beside them, "I am truly impressed by your effort and ingenuity. Why not swear the oath of loyalty to me, and forego your executions?"

"Why not?" West hissed. "Well, I guess maybe I'd rather see what happens when I stuff *you* into that cannon up there!"

Loveless wasn't too pleased with that answer. With one small tap of the button on his chair, a metal foot shot out and sent West crashing through the floor below him. West took a moment to get up, and when he did he noticed Loveless, in his wheelchair, rolling toward him down a ramp.

As Loveless sped closer, West jumped into the air, grabbed onto an overhead strut, reversed, and shoved the wheelchair off the ramp.

Loveless couldn't move. His wheels were firmly jammed.

He grinned, unfazed, then pushed another button and grinned again as four metal legs appeared from underneath the wheelchair, raising his body to a height of six foot ten.

"Now," he taunted, staring down at West. "Was it someone particularly close to you who perished in that military action?" He knew of course, just how to push Jim's buttons — remind him of his parents' cruel death.

West kicked him, aiming high, sending him spinning in his chair.

Using one of the metal legs, Loveless kicked him back, sending him sprawling.

"A mother, perhaps? A father?"

West glared, trying to get to his feet, when a cleated metal foot came down on his hand. He lay back, screaming in pain.

Gordon couldn't help him. The gun was still pointed at his head. All he could do was stand there and watch as the metal legs danced on his partner unmercifully.

After a moment Gordon couldn't stand it any longer, and he turned and threw out his arms to beg for his partner's life.

"Stop the violence!" he shouted as something cold and metallic flew out of his sleeve.

Gordon stared at it in amazement. He had forgotten about the gun. What was he going to do with it? He hated guns.

"Stop or I'll shoot!" he cried as West's eyes widened in amazement. Gordon shoot?

"You expect to kill me with that little peashooter?" Loveless laughed.

"If I have to, yes," Gordon replied, standing straight and tall.

Loveless looked down at Gordon and shrugged.

"Why is it that I am unafraid?" he asked. "I believe you gentlemen are polar opposites of a moral dilemma and I'm stuck in the middle. On one end, we have Mr. West, a man of primitive vigors uncomplicated by intellect. And on the other, there's Mr. Gordon, a man of ideas, but unlike myself he lacks the passion to kill for them."

Loveless's metal leg pushed down on West's head.

"Shoot him, Gordon!" West gasped.

A shot burst from Gordon's gun, startling everyone, including Gordon himself.

Loveless began to laugh. "After all that, you missed," he said.

But Gordon hadn't really missed. The shot had punctured a tube in one of the metal legs. A steady stream of hydraulic fluid was spraying out, covering the deck, rendering the foot on West's head powerless.

West slid away and got to his feet. "Better than a fountain pen, don't you think?" he asked his partner.

Gordon wasn't listening. He was gazing in the direction of Grant's finger. The President was pointing toward a hundred-foot cliff, his eyes wide with terror and confusion. Frantically, Gordon started pulling levers. This one. That one. But the tarantula continued on, moving closer and closer to the edge.

West went belowdeck. He was searching for Loveless. It was payback time. He found him shriveled in his chair, the metal legs collapsed below him.

"For almost four long years I've been tracking the animal responsible for the massacre at New Liberty. And I hear that's you," West said, staring down at him with hard eyes.

Loveless gazed up at him, begging for mercy, hoping to fool West into letting him

163

go. But West wasn't fooled, and when the guns popped out of Loveless's armrests he was ready. He leapt up and grabbed the I-beam over his head as Loveless pulled the triggers . . . and missed.

The bullets punctured the pipes behind West, spewing steam, just as Gordon and Grant, on the floor above, were preparing to die. The tarantula was at the edge of the cliff and there was no way they could stop it.

They didn't have to. Loveless's pipe-shots had stopped it for them, lurching them to a halt suddenly, so suddenly, in fact, that Loveless's chair began to roll, passing below West, toward the opposite railing.

As West hung there, watching it go, watching it hit a pool of hydraulic fluid and spin Loveless around 180 degrees, watching it continue on toward the abyss, he felt no sympathy. This was the man who had wiped out his family.

"You know, Loveless," he said, dropping

down, "it looks like I'm gonna finally be able to put the war behind me, and I think you should, too."

And with that he gave the wheelchair a small nudge with his boot and sent this man who had been haunting him for such a long time, Dr. Loveless, sailing over the cliff.

CHAPTER 20

They were back at Promontory Point, and the stake that would join the railroads together was finally in place.

As the crowd cheered, President Grant lowered the sledgehammer and turned to West and Gordon.

"Gentlemen," he said, "I now strongly believe the United States is going to be truly united. Not because of this railroad, but because of you."

Grant dug into his pocket and pulled out two silver shields.

"I have been thinking about extending the powers of the Secret Service. At this moment the Service guards us against counterfeiting and forgery. But I believe that Presidents need protection from lunatics like Loveless, so I am appointing you my guards."

President Grant leaned over and pinned the badges onto their vests.

"Welcome to the Secret Service, Body-Guards Number One and Two," he said as he shook their hands.

"Uh, just out of curiosity," Gordon said, trying to sound polite. "But which one of us is Agent Number One?"

The President rolled his eyes skyward.

"I don't think that matters very much, do you, Gordon?" he groaned. "Besides, you'll have plenty of time to discuss it on your new assignment. I'll see you in Washington."

He handed them a piece of paper, snapped a salute, and turned to go.

"But sir," Gordon said. "What about our train?"

"Well, I'm taking it, of course," Grant informed him over his shoulder. "You let Loveless blow mine up."

Gordon and West looked at each other in dismay as Rita came up behind them and tapped them on the shoulder.

"Rita! You look great!" West gushed.

"Ravishing!" Gordon agreed. "A vision!"

"I just wanted to thank you for everything you've done for me, before I go back home to Texas."

"Texas!" West cried. "Why don't you come to Washington with me!"

"Or better still," Gordon said, "come with *me* to Washington!"

But Rita shook her head at both of them.

"It's not that you both don't have your attributes," she told them. "You're so sophisticated and such a wonderful cook, Arte. And you're so good with a gun and have great legs, Jim. But I'm afraid I haven't been completely honest with you. Professor Escobar's not my father. He's my husband."

"Well, why didn't you just tell us that in the first place?" West asked indignantly.

"Would you really have brought me along if I'd said I was married?" Rita said. "I don't think so."

She started to walk away, then turned back and smiled at them.

"At least you still have each other," she said. And then she was gone.

West and Gordon were left alone.

"You know, Arte," West said.

"What's that, Jim?"

"Maybe Rita's right." They were perched on top of the tarantula, side by side, strutting off into the sunset together. "Besides, there's a lot of other women in this world."

"That's easy for you to say," Gordon said. "She didn't walk off with your best dress."